Notes *from the* Narrow Place

Notes *from the* Narrow Place

Essays and Stories
on Illness, Quarantine, and Healing

Philip Graubart

RESOURCE *Publications* · Eugene, Oregon

NOTES FROM THE NARROW PLACE
Essays and Stories on Illness, Quarantine, and Healing

Resource Publications
An Imprint of Wipf and Stock Publishers
199 W. 8th Ave., Suite 3
Eugene, OR 97401

www.wipfandstock.com

PAPERBACK ISBN: 978-1-6667-4204-6
HARDCOVER ISBN: 978-1-6667-4205-3
EBOOK ISBN: 978-1-6667-4206-0

JUNE 10, 2022 7:46 AM

For Susan

Contents

Acknowledgements

Many thanks to the following for publishing these pieces:

Tikkun published "Next Year in Silwan" and "Rise Up My Love."

Jewish Literary Journal published "The Wise Man of Chelm" and "On Hell Planet."

JewishFiction.Net published "Reb Moishe and the Beanstalks."

CCAR Journal published "Notes from the Narrow Place."

"Crowns" appears in *A God We Can Believe In* edited by Rifat Sonsino and Richard Agler.

Introduction

IN LATE WINTER 2019, I entered the narrow place. I mean that in two senses, which is to say I acquired two rooms in that place, two prison cells, both equally confining. One was the narrowness wrought by my physical and emotional symptoms. In a still mysterious case of what most of my many doctors (though not all) diagnosed as asthma, my lungs narrowed, which made it difficult to breathe. The same condition robbed me of sleep, inducing a bone-chilling fatigue that greatly narrowed my range of activities. Also, the physical symptoms, at least for the first several months as I journeyed down a rabbit hole of tests and procedures, generated a fear that crowded out most other emotions, to the point where if you asked how I was feeling on most days back then, the true answer would have been "afraid."

The other narrowness came when I retired from my job—a position that provided me a rich and full emotional and intellectual life, and which kept me hopping from classroom to boardroom to spiritual retreats, to Shabbat dinners, creative worship services, trips to Israel, not to mention tennis and basketball with high school students. That all stopped and was replaced with one set of activities: doctors' appointments, medical tests, wrestling with insurance companies and hospital accounting offices. Often the only person I would speak to on a given workday was a medical receptionist.

The biblical Hebrew word for "narrow place" is *meitzar*. It's from the same root as the Hebrew word for Egypt—*Mitzrayim*.

So when I say I entered the narrow place, what I really mean is that somehow I ended up a slave, back in Egypt. For a rabbi, that's traveling in the wrong direction.

One year later, in the early spring of 2020 the entire world joined me in the narrow place. The pandemic limited the physical places we could go. Our paths narrowed: home to grocery store, a walk around the block, bedroom to computer. The virus spawned worldwide fear, which narrowed the human emotional palette, often with disastrous consequences. And, of course, those with symptoms found their bronchial passages narrowed, and they struggled to breathe. Many succumbed to the ultimate narrow space—death. I can't say I was grateful for the company here in the narrow place, but our universal condition of confinement got me thinking about how the heart yearns for wide open spaces.

What does a rabbi do when he finds himself back in Egypt, the place where his entire religious tradition insists we left? What do we all do in a life that has suddenly shrunk? The answer for this particular rabbi is this book. In these pieces—fiction and non-fiction—I grapple with life in the narrow place, where choices disappear, but sometimes new ones emerge. Where certain types of physical activity cease but emotional and spiritual pursuits shoehorn their way into our lives, and we make room. Where we can sometimes find expansiveness, and even freedom back here in Egypt.

A word about genre. My whole writing life, I've used different forms to grapple with the same large issues of life, death, spirituality, ethics, identity, God, human relationships and more. I make up stories, or I interpret the Torah, or I probe my own memories for wisdom, not really caring or spending much time worrying about how I'm getting at the truth, only that I'm trying. So, although this collection contains memoir and exegesis and outright fiction— from my perspective it's all the same. These are my postcards from Egypt, notes from my narrow place.

Part One

ESSAYS

Chapter One

Rise Up My Love

THE LAST TIME I saw Christine, she brought me a four-foot layer cake. Three of the four feet were a blue and white sugar sculpture likeness of my smiling face. She limped into my office, holding the cake on a cardboard tray. She seemed about to trip, so I jumped up and eased the vanilla monstrosity on to my office coffee table, while she tumbled into a chair.

"Happy Birthday," she said, catching her breath.

I stared at my sugar face, then answered, logically, "It's not my birthday." This was January; my birthday's in July.

"Well, I don't know your birthday." She turned to the cake. "But this is part of my final assignment—a personalized birthday cake. You can probably tell, I based it on your bio photo."

I have a bio photo? I thought. I looked at the strange smiling figure, which did in fact look a lot like me. Except for something in the smile I couldn't pinpoint. "It's not quite me, is it?" I said.

"Oh, well, I filled in the gap in your teeth." She took out her phone and showed me the photo from my installation as rabbi at Beth El. I was more than ten years younger, and not totally gray—another detail in my favor. She'd photoshopped better teeth.

"Ah. I knew I didn't look that good." I smiled at her, but kept my teeth hidden.

Christine was finishing up a course in cake decoration. After three years of social work, following her graduation from the

University of California in San Diego, she was bravely embarking on a new career. We'd been close when I was supervising her conversion to Judaism, meeting every other week, sharing theologies, debating biblical and rabbinic texts. But in the past few years, she'd attended Chai events, our young adult program led by our associate rabbi, so I didn't see her that often. I was touched that my younger, smiling, teeth-repaired face made it to one of her cake-decorating assignments.

"But really, I just came here because I wanted to hear the song?" She looked at my Taylor acoustic guitar, stashed in the corner of the office. "Can you, please?"

I watched her touch the bottom of her neck as she spoke. I studied her worried face, her long blond hair, her thin arms. "Are you okay?"

She nodded, forced a smile, but didn't speak. I reached for my guitar.

Christine had a rare genetic disorder that affected her circulatory system and especially her lungs. As a child, she'd been hospitalized and intubated several times. She walked with a limp, could only speak when covering a hole in her throat, and was perhaps the thinnest person I'd ever met. And she was transcendentally beautiful, radiant, joyful, loving and wise. She spoke easily about her mortality. In our first conversation, she told me "I want to live to be 99, like my great grandmother. But no one expected me to survive my thirteenth birthday. So I guess every day is a blessing." I googled her disease and consulted a few doctors I knew, but the condition was so rare, I couldn't find a solid prognosis. She was sick, infirm, limited. But she lived a full life. She'd either continue and live a long time, or she wouldn't. Either was possible.

I played the song, "Arise My Love." She often requested I sing it for her. Lately, it was our only interaction. She'd pop in, ask me to play the song, listen, sometimes dance a kind of wounded ballet, her small feet shuffling oddly while her skinny arms swayed in imprecise time. She'd smile widely, showing perfect teeth. Then, when I finished, she'd limp away. That day—the cake day—was the last time I played it for her in person.

I first saw her sitting in the back corner of the sanctuary with a group of young friends. Christine wore a sleeveless yellow dress which highlighted her bony arms. Her blond hair flowed nearly to her waist. The rest of her crowd—two men, two women—sported clean pressed jeans and button-down shirts: college semi-formal. They arrived together at 9:40 AM, 10 minutes late for the beginning of Shabbat services, but quite early for synagogue etiquette, where the bulk of congregants showed up between 10 and 10:30. At first I assumed they were non-Jews, coming for a bar mitzvah, or a baby-naming or a pre-wedding ceremony. It was certainly not normal for five college-age folk to attend services. They brought the average age of the regulars down 10 or 15 points. Guests, I figured. But I remembered there was no celebration scheduled for that day, and I noticed they picked up the correct books from the shelves in front of them and sang along like shul veterans. I tried to reach them after services, but they scooted out before the end of *Adon Olam*. They came the next week, and then the next several Saturday mornings in a row, each time exiting during the final hymn. Naturally, they were the talk of the synagogue at the *kiddush* refreshment table. "Maybe they're saying *kaddish*?" one elderly lady suggested. But none of them stood for the prayer. "An Introduction to World Religion class assignment?" another man offered. But that wouldn't go on for six weeks. Besides, these young people knew what they were doing. The men wore their extra large *tallises* with the exact correct folds. All five bowed and stepped and swayed and rose and sat at the right times, before being prompted by me. They knew the difference between the two books in the pews. They all stretched to touch the Torah as we processed it around the room, and then kissed either their *tallises* (the men), or their prayerbooks (the women). And they sang—quietly, but correctly. We were left with the unlikely, yet unmistakable conclusion that they were here to pray. A retired professor confirmed it for us. He'd seen them at UCSD Hillel, the Jewish campus organization. They were undergraduates. But why were they praying here?

Finally, their seventh week in the pews, they stayed for the entirety of *Adon Olam*, and approached me afterwards as a group. Christine, in her yellow dress, slouched behind the others and looked down. Her blond hair partially covered her face. "Do you do conversions?" a young man asked me, wearing jeans, glasses, and a white shirt.

I was confused. Of all of them, this guy seemed the most familiar with Jewish customs. He'd even accepted the offer of an *aliyah* to the Torah, where he deployed his *tallis* expertly while kissing the parchment and recited the prayer from memory. "You're converting?" I asked. He glanced behind his shoulder, as if asking for permission to continue.

"He's asking for me," Christine said, brushing her hair out of her face. She pointed to her friends. "They're all here for me."

And that was the last time she seemed at all shy.

The next day, she hobbled into my office and told me her story. She was raised as a Messianic Jew, a Christian sect formerly known as "Jews for Jesus," which aped certain Jewish rituals and festivals but embraced Jesus as their master, teacher, messiah, and son of God. When she said the words "Messianic Jew," she reared back, as if expecting me to slap her. But I just nodded. She smiled, a crooked, knowing smile, as if we were sharing a naughty joke. "Wow, I thought you'd flip out. That's why I insisted we leave early every week. I was too scared to talk with you. Whenever I remind Joel that I'm a Jew for Jesus, he balls up his fists. I'm glad you're staying calm."

Actually, I wasn't undisturbed by the concept. Most Jews I know distrust the perversely contradictory idea of a Jew for Jesus. But I really knew nothing about Messianic Jewish communities— their structure, their "synagogues"—and I was intrigued by this dynamic, young, physically damaged college student.

"It started with a dream. I can't even remember how old I was. Young. Three maybe four. Not my first memory, but one of the first. Maybe the first memory of a dream. But old enough that I knew that I was a cripple. That it hurt to walk, that other people could walk better than me. I dreamt that an angel touched me and took away my pain. I could walk. I say angel, but it didn't look like an angel. It looked like, well, like a rabbi. Sort of like you, but more rabbi-like, you know? With a long gray beard and a black coat. A, what do you call those hats? A big black hat. And a beautiful smile. I cried when I woke up, because I realized it was a just a dream, that I was still a hunchbacked cripple. I guess I was old enough to understand the difference between dreams and reality. My mom heard me crying and ran in, so I told her the dream. 'Oh, it was Jesus,' she said. 'Jesus came to you in a dream and promised to heal you.' Well, that just pissed me off, because that wasn't the dream. There wasn't any promise. And it certainly wasn't Jesus. I mean, the guy was old and overweight. In a good way. 'It was an angel of God,' I said, but then, wide awake, I realized it couldn't have been an angel. I knew angels had wings, were all white, and this was some chuckling, kind, chubby guy with a gray beard and black hat, and a *tallis*. 'I mean it was God,' I told my mother. 'Not Jesus, God.'"

Christine stopped, shook her head, and asked for water. I ran to the staff room, grabbed a bottle and hurried back. I found her limping among my bookshelves, lingering beside the Hebrew volumes—the Talmud, Maimonides, the *Shulkhan Aruch*. She plucked out a book, a Hasidic commentary on Genesis, and slowly ran a finger along the Hebrew letters. "You can read this," she said, a statement, not a question.

I handed her the bottle of water. She drained it in two gulps, then sat down. She took a deep breath. I couldn't tell if she was nervous or just easily winded. "It wasn't Jesus," she said. "In my dream."

"I understand."

She laughed. "I'm not sure you do. I still don't. When I say it wasn't Jesus, I don't mean that Jesus didn't happen to be a character in my dream. His absence was like a presence, you know? Discernable. Like when you're in pain, and it suddenly stops. You feel it—the absence of pain."

I nodded and tried to remember the last time I'd experienced a great physical pain that suddenly stopped. I'm not sure that had ever happened to me.

"It's like there had been this barrier. This wall, this enclosure. And it disappeared. I'd been confined. And now I wasn't. I was free."

"You were 3-years-old?"

She laughed. I saw now that she laughed easily, contagiously, and often the focus of her laughter was something odd about herself. She enjoyed her own foibles; they amused her. "My whole life, I've thought about God. I don't remember a time when I didn't. So, yeah, even at 3, or maybe it was 4, I noticed that it was God who took away my pain, and not Jesus. That Jesus *not* being there was part of the experience." She looked at me. It was my turn to say something. I was the rabbi, the religion expert.

"Jesus had blocked you," I said. "Stopped you from getting to God."

"Stopped me from praying to God for healing. Stopped me from healing."

I watched her move her hair away from her face, a consistent tic. I considered not bringing up an obvious flaw in her reasoning, but forged ahead. "But are you healed?"

She laughed, touched her throat. "Do I look healed?"

That's when she gave me her medical history, including a discouraging prognosis, which she presented calmly, almost humorously, as if her illness were a kind of cosmic joke. When she finished she turned her gaze to my bookshelves. "I don't necessarily expect God to heal me," she said. "But if He did, it would be God, not Jesus. Does that make any sense?"

It was as coherent a theology as I'd ever heard. "It does," I said.

"So I can convert with you?"

A bright undergraduate who gracefully transcended an obvious handicap, and who couldn't remember ever not thinking about God? Most candidates for conversion entered the process because they were engaged to Jews—a good enough reason, and I was always happy to help. But Christine was seeking to clarify her relationship with God, her life of prayer. Her goal was liberation, breaking through her perceived spiritual confinement. "I'd be honored," I told her.

After that, she became a "candidate." In a "program." I had an unusually high number of people converting that year—10; our associate rabbi had another 10—and with the busy schedule of a senior rabbi in a large congregation, I couldn't devote much time to any of them. Like her fellow converts, Christine read *The Nine Question People Ask About Judaism* by Dennis Prager and Joseph Telushkin, *The Jewish Holidays* by Michael Strassfeld, *Living a Jewish Life*, by Anita Diament. For her theology book she chose *Standing Again at Sinai* by Judith Plaskow. She kept a journal of her Jewish experiences. She continued to attend services with her college crew on Saturday mornings.

I met with her every two weeks. She'd read to me from her journal; describe how putting on tefillin made her feel tied up ("Not doing that again!"); how sometimes when she lit the Shabbat candles she felt herself ascending with the flames ("Not in a good way, or bad way, it just felt natural, like I'd become the flame"), and how she really didn't enjoy our synagogue music ("You could do *so* much better. Just go to one Messianic service, just for the music"). Every so often, perhaps every third visit, she looked paler than usual, more gaunt, and seemed to struggle more than before getting up from her chair. I'd ask her if she was okay, and she'd smile and wave me off. "Couldn't be better," she said, and I couldn't tell if it was seasoned cynicism, or true strength and courage, or both. Or faith. After a few visits, I stopped noticing that she touched her throat every time she talked.

One afternoon, she caught me singing and playing guitar. It was late March, and I was preparing for a creative Passover Seder. I needed to practice the song "Arise My Love," by Debbie Friedman, and, as Christine had pointed out about me and our synagogue music, we could use some improvement. So I was playing loudly, trying to find exactly the right tune, and I didn't hear her walk in. I was just finishing the final coda ("Rise up my love, my fair one. And come away. And come away. And come away.") when I looked up and nearly dropped my guitar. Christine was dancing—ballet-like movements, awkward with her limps, but rhythmically interesting. And her grin—the pale light from her face—lit up the room. Embarrassed, I put down the guitar.

"No, no," she said, still shuffling her small feet, still grinning. "You can't stop. I need you to play that song again."

"Okay. Can you, uh, sit while I play?"

"No, I can't," she said.

I nodded and played the song, a setting for the biblical book "Song of Songs." She swayed slowly, but joyfully while I played.

Rise up my love my fair one. And come away.
For lo the winter is here and the rain has come.
The flowers appear on Earth. The time of singing has come.
And the voice of the turtle dove is heard.
The fig tree bringeth forth its fresh green figs.
And the vines in blossom, they bring forth fragrance.
Arise, arise my love, my fair one come away.
Arise my love and come away.
Rise up my love my fair one. And come away. And come away.
And come away.

═══

By the final coda, tears dampened her cheeks. She was clearly moved, even with my bumbling out-of-tune performance (remember, I needed practice). I hesitated asking her why the song made her cry. Was it romance? I wondered. Most converting students were marrying Jews, but certainly not all, and Christine never mentioned a boyfriend or girlfriend. With her physical condition, it would be difficult to carry on a romantic relationship, but certainly not impossible. Finally, I just asked. "Why the tears, Christine?"

She shook her head, as if denying the obvious wetness on her cheeks. She hadn't stopped smiling since she walked in the room. "She's flying away," she said. "She's rising up. She's becoming free."

I nodded.

She sat, and I put away my guitar. "Who wrote that?" she asked.

I told her it was from "Song of Songs." Biblical love poems.

She paused for a second, then put her finger on her throat. "But it's about God, right? That's what we learned in my synagogue. Well, I mean my church. We called it a synagogue." She laughed.

"Some people interpret it that way. That it's about God. A metaphor. God's the man; the Jewish people are the woman. Or, I guess maybe you learned that Jesus was the man."

"Of course," she said, remembering, contemplating. "But I never saw it that way. Oh, but it's definitely a metaphor. It's about God. I mean, just listen to how you sang it."

I told her I wouldn't rely on how I sing for anything. "But I have to say, to me, it doesn't read like a metaphor. Some of the images are purely erotic."

She giggled. "Look, let me just show you." She looked around my office. "Do you have a bible in here?"

I had dozens of shelves filled with bibles and biblical commentary. I took out the Jewish Publication Society's Hebrew-English Tanach and handed it to her. She flipped quickly to Song of Songs and pointed to some verses in Chapter 3. "I sought the one I love—I sought but found him not." "See," Christine said, "she's craving a relationship with God, but there's all these barriers." She recited some more. "'I met the watchmen.' These guardians, she runs into them. That's the Church, religious establishments, it's everyone trying to keep God for themselves." She flipped ahead a few pages. "Here's Chapter 5. Listen to this. 'I opened the door for my beloved. But my beloved had turned and gone.' Every time she gets close to embracing her beloved—God—something happens. Poof, He's gone. Then, listen, she meets the watchmen again. 'I met the watchmen who patrol the town. They struck me, they bruised me.' All these obstacles. Church establishments throwing rules at her. Her own laziness. Physical weakness. But all through the book, she keeps trying. She's desperate to find God."

I stared at her. I'd never met anyone who actually believed the metaphoric reading of Song of Songs, who'd ever internalized the idea that God could be a passionate lover, and that humans could love God with an erotic intensity. The notion had always disturbed me, ruined for me the exquisite poetry of Song of Songs. But Christine, with her wounded body, and sensitive soul, demonstrated for me the power of her reading. She danced to it.

"There's something else about Song of Songs," she said. "You asked why I was crying."

It looked to me like she was *still* crying. Her cheeks shone with tears, though her near constant smile decorated her face. She picked up the bible, stared at a page, then put the book down. "I thought of something while you were singing." She smiled. "I realized the girl in the song is not stuck. Not completely. Play the first line."

My fingers formed a C chord. I played the first line.

"'Rise up my love,'" she repeated. "The way you sing it—not just you, the melody—it sounds like it's possible. Like she could rise up. She could fly. She's flying inside; trapped and flying at the same time. For me, Song of Songs was always about the struggle. I admired the sentiments. It's not easy to love God. You have to go through so much pain to get to the love. But the song focuses on transcendence." She smiled and flapped her arms, her wings. "'Arise.'"

"'Come away,'" I said.

"The fig tree. It's blooming. Vines are opening up. I don't know why I never noticed. It's not just about the barriers. It's about transcendence."

"Freedom?" I suggested. "You know, we recite it on Passover."

She nodded. "Of course. Freedom, sure. But for me? It's about flying."

We looked at each other, two students, finding new meaning in an ancient text. I could see she was lost in thought, rolling the lyrics around in her mind. "I asked you who wrote it."

I told her scholars weren't sure. Jewish tradition claimed it was King Solomon.

"No," she laughed. "I don't mean who wrote the Bible. I meant the melody."

I thought for a moment, then remembered, astonished that I would have forgotten. I told her about Debbie Friedman.

Debbie was the singer laureate of American Judaism, the artist who transformed Jewish liturgical music from European high art opera to Simon and Garfunkel/Peter Paul and Mary style folk music. If you went to Jewish summer camp, or attended Jewish youth groups, or even just showed up at services occasionally, her songs were everywhere. They were choreographed, with canonical handclaps, tambourine shakes.

Also, she suffered from a cruel neurological disorder which robbed her of her ability to perform and eventually killed her. Before her final disintegration, she gave several searingly moving talks about living with illness, transcending physical barriers, flying free from your body. Her healing song became the emotional highlight of many non-Orthodox services, not necessarily because of the folky melody, but because most of us knew her story.

I told Christine about Debbie, expecting her to smile with recognition. Debbie hadn't yet died, so I figured Christine would see her as a heroine, a role model. Instead, she looked pensive and nodded. "Uh huh," she said. "Do you mind playing the song again." I played it again. She cried then laughed.

=====

Christine finished her conversion studies. For her ritual immersion, we drove to La Jolla shores on a cool, foggy June morning (when you move to La Jolla, nobody tells you how cold it gets in June). She limped across the sand with her college buddies, rubbing her thin arms against the morning chill. It was 6AM; we wanted to get there before the surfers took over. She took several quick breaths, then sprinted into the water, her limp slowing her down not at all. When she'd swum 20-some feet into the waves, she slipped off her one-piece red bathing suit, and immersed herself three times, in three quick practiced moves. She was Jewish. Five minutes later, shivering, wrapped in three towels, she sang the Shma. She chose the Debbie Friedman melody.

Then she disappeared. I don't mean literally. She remained an active part of the congregation, particularly the young adult social/religious group we called Chai. By "disappeared" I mean we didn't see each other on a regular basis. There were no more bi-weekly pre-conversion meetings in my office where we debated God language, sang songs while I played guitar, and she'd dance her wounded dance, twirling like an angel. When someone as vital and light as Christine stops meeting with you every other Thursday, it feels like a disappearance. Her absence becomes a presence. But, of course, I was pleased. Christine fit into the community the way she fit into Judaism—perfectly, like she'd always been there, like the synagogue and the religion had been designed with her in mind. Christine and her band of college students, eventually young grads, became as familiar a part of the sanctuary on Saturdays as the old regulars, as the Torah, as the ark.

═══

I thought about Christine quite a bit after I got sick with a lung ailment, eight years after she converted. "She's flying inside," she'd told me, about the young lover in "Song of Songs." Transcending the watchmen who struck her, flying above her own laziness and indecisiveness, the taunts of other maidens. One night when my lungs wouldn't let me sleep, I took a well-worn *Tanach* down from the shelf and leafed through "Song of Songs." The first four chapters left me cold. I couldn't get past the mushy eroticism, the "kisses of your mouth," "breasts sweeter than wine," "bundle of myrrh, my lover for me, between my breasts." Not what I, an old, sick guy, was looking for in the middle of the night. I struggled to remember why the book had so moved Christine, energized her into dancing her wounded ballet. Then I came to Chapter 5, and something clicked. "I am asleep but my heart awakes." I yawned. Fatigued beyond mercy, but somehow still awake. Ill, but still somehow, fully alive. "My beloved knocks. 'Open for me! My sister, my love.'" Open, I thought. The thirst for openness, for expanses. I took a breath, opened my lungs. I remembered a line from Psalms, which also appears in the morning prayer service: "You've opened my sackcloth and robed me in joy." I exhaled, freely. The move from mourning to joy was also the move from constriction to openness. I reached for a *siddur* and found the prayer—Psalm 96. My eyes landed on the verse preceding the line about opening my sackcloth: "You've transformed my mourning into my dancing." Confinement—sackcloth and mourning—becomes movement, dance, flight. Christine could feel that transformation every time she got out of bed and limped into her day. She flew on the inside.

Back to "Song of Songs," Chapter 5. The man calls to his would-be lover from the other side of the door "Open for me!" She reaches for the doorknob. She "opens" it.

But her beloved has disappeared. She fights her way to him, past the wicked watchmen, the jealous friends ("How is your beloved better than others?"). She seems to find him; he's "gone down to his garden, he "browses among the lilies." But then he's gone, or she's changed her mind. He cries out to her, "Come my beloved, let us go to the field, let us lie in the vineyards." I realized the whole book follows this pattern: yearning, closure, then openness and freedom, then loss, then more yearning. That's how Christine lived day to day. Yearning, then fighting for freedom, for expanses, for dancing. Then, once again, the harsh reality of her body closing down. And then again freedom. That was also Debbie Friedman's dance. I saw her perform twice when friends led her nearly crippled body up onto the stage. But somehow the music, her music, opened her up, filled her, the hall, and all our hearts. Her sackcloth became joy. Could I do that? I wondered. I wasn't as sick as Christine or Debbie. I didn't need as much "opening up," meaning I didn't need as much faith. But was I as strong?

I asked the same question not long afterwards, in the pandemic's early months, but this time I asked it about all of us—Americans, humans. We, who were stuck inside, hiding from a different illness, quarantined, yearning for doors to open, longing for the masks to fall from our faces, hungry for the wide-open spaces outside our homes. Somehow, we found the openings, the cracks in the quarantine. Dinner parties moved to virtual spaces.

Education went online. Where before we would have transcended time and space with our cars and shopped at the mall, we walked around the block in the fresh air. We filled our ears with exquisite, expansive ideas and gorgeous music broadcast from wallet-sized devices. We reunited on Zoom with cousins we hadn't seen in years; we played computer games with old friends who lived miles and miles away. The world narrowed, but also expanded. The watchmen– not just the virus, but a rancid politics, racist violence, and endless fear—beat us down. As of this writing, we still oscillate between shutdowns and re-openings. But we persevere, we hear the knock on the door, we reach to open it, we imagine the spaces outside, and we fly on the inside.

By the time the pandemic hit, I'd managed to find new spaces in my lungs, enough for long walks, and then short jogs, and even bike rides. My condition didn't change, but the inspiration Debbie and Christine bequeathed to me gave me the skill of dancing with what I have. It's a limping, wounded dance, but it's saved my life. For me, the virus was one more watchman, beating me down. But I did what I could to dance away.

The day after Christine delivered the cake decorated with my improved face, I heard that Debbie Friedman had passed away at the age of 58. I never met her personally. But the Jewish world being what it is, especially the world of Jewish professionals, I knew people who knew her. And of course, the entire American Jewish community mourned. Sitting alone in my office, I choked back tears. I wondered if I should call Christine. Ten minutes later she called. She was too sick to make it to the office and didn't want to trouble me with a visit. She just wanted to hear the song. I played it for her over the phone. I didn't tell her about Debbie, and we never spoke about her death. But of course, she knew. The whole Jewish world knew.

Two weeks later, Christine called me at 9 PM, late for her, and for me. "I think it's more serious this time."

"I'm coming over," I told her.

"No, no, that's not why I called. I appreciate the offer. I've got company. That's not the issue. I'm asking you not to."

"Okay."

"I just, I think it might be—no, never mind. I'm feeling better."

"Really?"

"I just . . . I think . . . well, one day it will be more serious. It will be, you know, the serious one."

"I know," I said.

"I need it to be a Jewish ceremony, okay? I'm not sure my parents . . . well, just, that's what I want. Okay?"

I offered to come over again. She laughed. "I told you I'm better. This time. I'm up. I'm dancing. Just promise me."

I promised. A Jewish service. I didn't want to say the word funeral.

Back then, I didn't indulge much in private prayer. I led services, four days a week, and stuck to the many benedictions and requests in the formal Jewish liturgy. In those pre-lung disease, pre-pandemic times, that had always seemed sufficient. But that night I made what I thought was a reasonable and humble request. I don't want her to die, I told God. She's too young. And too marvelous and strong and open. I'm calling you from the depths, I wept before God. From the narrow place. Keep Christine alive.

She died anyway. Two days later. She was 26.

No arguments with her parents about the service. No arguments with them at all; they could barely utter sounds. They looked like two people who had wandered into an alternate reality, where, bizarrely, parents outlive their adult children. Their faces expressed both horror and a deep, impatient puzzlement, as if they were expecting, any minute, for the person in charge to show up and explain to them, in their native tongue, that it was all a mistake. I'd seen the expression before. I'm a rabbi. I'm familiar with grief. But I'd glimpsed it that morning, briefly, in my own bathroom mirror.

Three of Christine's young friends spoke at the funeral. I don't remember much of what they said. The world is a darker place, a tall burly man with a colorful yarmulke said. I nodded. It was, I thought. And narrower. More confining.

Christine's uncle, her father's brother, spoke the longest. He told a story I'll never forget. He reminded us that Christine had been sick most of her life, and she always understood the severity of her illness. One particularly cruel episode struck her when she was 13. Bat mitzvah age, he said, and glanced at me. She was stuck in the hospital for months. Her lungs worked hard, harder than a pale, skinny child's lungs should ever have to work, but still not quite hard enough. She was connected to several tubes, including a ventilator. One difficult morning, the uncle cornered Christine's father and said, "You have to ask her. Is this what she wants? Does she want to keep fighting? Has she had enough? You have to at least find out what she wants." Christine's father nodded. They went into the hospital room together and asked the nurses and technicians to leave. Christine couldn't talk, but her nurse had set up a handheld light for communication: two lights for yes, one for no. Her father took her by the hand and said, "Honey, I just have to know. Do you want to keep fighting?"

They waited. Tears formed in Christine's 13-year-old, bat mitzvah-age eyes. One light blinked on. One meant no. But then, another light. She'd answered yes. She kept fighting. She fought for 13 more years. I've been flashing those two lights for several years now, even after retiring for health reasons. In my worst moments, Christine's answer brightens the gloom.

After Christine's uncle, it was my turn to speak. I had a few notes prepared, but really, I didn't want to talk. Instead, I picked up my guitar and walked slowly to the podium. My fingers found the familiar C chord, and I strummed once or twice. "This is a song Christine loved," I said. I took a deep breath, filling up all the narrow spaces in my lungs, expanding them with air, precious air. "Rise up my love, my fair one," I sang. "And come away."

Chapter Two

Next Year in Silwan

Note: Some names and identifying details in this piece have been changed.

THE LAST TIME I saw Rafik, I was afraid he might stab me. Strange, because our surroundings seemed eminently genteel and civilized. Rafik was wearing a well-fitted black suit, white shirt, and maroon tie—a sharp contrast to my jeans and t-shirt. We sat in the hotel's VIP lounge, the elite spot in an already expensive restaurant. The napkins were cloth, the silver polished, and the tuxedoed waiters deferential to the point of superciliousness. That made sense— Rafik was their boss, the corporate Vice President whose thick portfolio of responsibilities included managing the hotel's menial labor force. I'd bonded with Rafik more than 30 years before, when both he and I cleaned bathrooms together at this same hotel, now renamed and fancier. But I'd moved away, graduated rabbinical school, built a career as an American rabbi. He'd stayed and climbed the hotel career ladder. When we scrubbed toilets and stripped sheets together, we never would have been allowed anywhere near the fancy dining room where we now ate sole Florentine, chicken kabobs, mint salad and drank lemonade. But here we were, in our

50s, with our strikingly divergent career paths, enjoying the luxury of a place that exploited and employed us when we were young.

Rafik was pissed off. I could tell by a sudden widening of his eyes, as if he'd just seen something shocking; a flash of red in his cheeks; and a pencil-thin line connecting his tightly pursed lips. I'd only seen that expression on him once, 15 years before, when, after a relatively happy reunion, he walked me through the small Jewish enclave that had sprouted up in his Arab neighborhood, a little more than a block from his house. Back then, I'd reassured him of my total sympathy, even though he talked so quickly I could barely understand what he was saying. This time, I'd asked about his wife and children, and that was enough to remind him of his family's home, and trigger the old anger.

We were in the middle of a war. Missiles from Gaza landed in Jerusalem, Israeli bombers leveled neighborhoods in Gaza, and Palestinian terrorists, mostly from the West Bank, were stabbing random Jews in different parts of the city. Rafik and I were dining in the lap of luxury, two educated, successful, civilized friends, but I couldn't help noticing how tightly he gripped his butter knife.

=====

I met Rafik in 1980. I was on my junior year abroad, studying at the Hebrew University's One Year Program. A friend of mine and I got lost on a *Footloose in Jerusalem* city walk through the Mount of Olives and decided to check out what looked like an interesting Arab neighborhood, what we later learned was Silwan. We climbed down a slope across from the Hill of Evil Counsel and entered a narrow cobblestone sidewalk that led us to a warren of winding streets and walkways, enclosed by tall Arab-style houses. Young boys kicked soccer balls, played tag, or tossed rocks at the houses and each other. They ignored us. We spotted a tall Arab woman, covered head to toe in multi-colored scarves and a long black and white dress, carrying a tray of fresh pita on her head. She must have noticed our staring, because she somehow managed to grab two pitas and toss them at us, smiling and nodding. We thanked her in Hebrew, and then my friend remembered one of the few Arab words he'd learned and said "*Shukran.*" "*B'vakashah,*" she responded, sticking to Hebrew. Just then, a lanky young man in black jeans, sneakers, and a red polo shirt stepped around the corner. He muttered a few quick words in Arabic to the woman—we soon learned she was his mother. She nodded. "You will have lunch at my house," he instructed us in what sounded to me like Jamaican-accented English. My friend and I looked at each other. We were 20 years old (so, it turned out, was Rafik). We were explorers. The Jewish parts of Israel had exotic elements, but we were getting used to those. The Arab areas offered extra stimulation for two adventure-starved suburban American Jews. "We will have lunch with you," my friend agreed. "*Shukran,*" I said.

The lunch turned out to be the best meal we'd had in Israel, one of the best meals I've had in my life. In addition to piles of fresh pita, Rafik's mother laid out six types of salads, with beets, tomatoes, cucumbers, potatoes, and some vegetables I didn't recognize. This was in addition to the several large plates of swirling hummus with olive oil and pine nuts, and tahina. Then came the kebabs—chicken, beef, mixed grill, lamb. We sat on the floor, on soft cushions, and leaned our backs against the light blue wall. It was late summer, hot and sunny in Jerusalem, but mystifyingly cool in Rafik's house.

We talked about books. It was a hard subject to ignore, since apart from the food and seat cushions, the room was covered in books. Not bookshelves—just books, piled floor to ceiling, a dozen book towers, side by side, surrounding us. I felt like a giant in some strange skyscraper-filled downtown.

"You like books?" Rafik asked.

I shrugged. At that point in my life, I didn't have much to say about books. "Sure," I said.

"English books?"

My friend and I looked at each other. "That's the only kind we can read," I said.

"So you will teach me?" Rafik asked.

I glanced around the room. I noticed that all the volumes were in English. I recognized the names of some authors. Mark Twain. Henry James. Dickens. Shakespeare. They seemed to be mostly fiction, classical works I only would have read if assigned, and even then, I was likely to prefer Cliff Notes. "Teach you to read?" I asked.

He laughed. "You think I can't read English? No, teach me about books. What else should I read? To help me with my English. And to improve myself."

Improve his English? As far as I could tell, he spoke it flawlessly. I was about to tell him when his mother came in with a golden pitcher and a tray of cookies. She poured coffee into tiny silver cups, nodded at us, smiling, then walked out. I noticed she walked with a slight limp.

"She has a whore head," Rafik said.

I looked at my friend. "Excuse me?" he said.

"A whore head," Rafik repeated. He touched his black hair. "You know. Uh, white. White hair. She is old, not walking properly. A hoar head."

He meant "gray-haired," meaning old. At the time, I'd never encountered the expression "hoar head." Later my friend looked it up. We chuckled as he read the scene in the King James translation of the Bible where David warns his son Solomon not to let Joab's "hoar head" die peacefully. In other words, kill him before he gets old, before his hair turns gray. "He learned English from random great books," my friend said.

At that first lunch, I agreed to suggest titles for him to read. On my next visit—this time I came by myself—I brought my paperback editions of The Foundation trilogy by Isaac Asimov. The books seemed smart, but plain spoken, an antidote to too much Shakespeare. The next time, I stopped in an English-language bookstore, and bought four novels by Hemingway. As plain spoken as you can get, I thought. I also wrote him letters, describing, in the best English I could muster, my university courses, or my impressions of Israel, or my heady experiences with women, or my thoughts on the upcoming American elections. He wrote back in grammatically perfect, stilted English, though I noticed as the year went by his style shifted from 19th-century intellectual to 20th century. More Hemingway, less Henry James.

My American friend lost interest, but I continued the visits, at least once a month. His mother cooked elaborate Middle Eastern meals—I later learned the family owned a restaurant/catering business—and we talked about books. One time I brought my then-girlfriend. That was the first time Rafik ventured with us out of his neighborhood. He showed us a hole in the security fence surrounding the Mt. Scopus Hebrew University campus. "Very easy to break into this Israeli place," he said, ducking under the barbed wire. "A good shortcut for you. Easy as cake," he said.

"Pie," I corrected. "Easy as pie."

"Pie, pie, pie," he said laughing, delighted, but also clearly disappointed with himself. "Such a funny, difficult language."

I wondered then, as I'd often wonder in the future, why he didn't attend Hebrew University, why he contented himself with sneaking under the fence, instead of enrolling, and entering through the front gate. He was clearly bright enough—he was one of the smartest people I'd ever met. But for some reason I was afraid to stray into personal topics, as if making friends with Rafik wasn't the point, the point was further adventures, getting to know a real Arab, learning about holes in fences. That year, I didn't share intimacies with Rafik, didn't reveal much of my personal life, and didn't ask about his.

That came two years later, when I returned to Israel for what I thought would be Aliyah, immigration. I enrolled in a graduate program at Hebrew University, reunited with a few friends, and found an apartment in the Germany Colony, at the time a relatively cheap, obscure neighborhood. My third week back, after eating dinner alone at one of the Hebrew University's many cafeterias, I hiked downhill to Silwan, wound my way through the twisting streets, and knocked on the door of his tall house. I'd been a poor correspondent, waiting months to answer his letters. But I thought of Rafik often and was curious what he was up to. His mother answered the door. She smiled widely, greeted me in Hebrew, then called Rafik in Arabic. He rushed to the door, hugged me tightly, and kissed me on both cheeks. "My best friend," he said. "You are so welcome here."

He sounded more Chicago than Jamaica. I wondered if he'd been watching American TV. We settled on the floor cushions and sipped the Turkish coffee that his mother brought. I told him I was back to stay. He nodded, approving. "You have a job," he said. I shook my head. "No, I'm a full-time student. I have a student visa. I don't think I'm even allowed to work."

He interrupted me. "No, no. Not a question. A statement. You have a job. I am giving you a job. You will need a job, no? For money. So you don't beg from your wealthy parents?"

My parents, of course, were not wealthy, at least not by American standards. But by that point, I was beginning to get Rafik's deadpan humor, his subtle exaggerations, the way he never laughed when he joked around. I'd planned to live frugally off my savings. I hadn't thought about a job. But Rafik insisted. "You have a job," he repeated.

The job was in a hotel—in *meshekh bayit*, housekeeping. Rafik had a family connection with the kitchen director. It was a new hotel, desperate for workers and willing to pay foreigners in cash, under the table. For six months, I teamed up with Rafik, scrubbing toilets, vacuuming rugs, sweeping up cigarette butts from non-smoking rooms, tossing out used condoms, and pocketing tips.

I hesitate to say we became close in those months, although sponging away vomit with a partner can create camaraderie. I never invited Rafik to my apartment in the German Colony, partly because I wasn't sure how he'd feel seeing my Arab house in a formerly Palestinian neighborhood. I didn't even consider introducing him to my mother, brother and sisters when they came to visit. I never met his father, or, for that matter, anyone in his family other than his mother, or any of his friends from the neighborhood. I didn't learn about his family business for another 10 years. I will say, with some mix of shame and pride, that it was while we cleaned bathrooms together that I stopped seeing him as "my Palestinian friend," a fascinating, exotic touristy leftover from my year abroad. He became, instead, a valued colleague, an interesting friend, someone I cared about, whose company I enjoyed, regardless of his ethnicity.

Oh, and we got high together, at least once a week, on the roof of his house, after work on Thursdays, and sometimes on Saturdays. He supplied the hashish. I never asked where he got it. While stoned beyond anything I'd ever encountered (and would ever encounter again), we engaged in some of the deepest conversation I'd ever enjoyed. We discussed the possibility of alien life, of the Fermi paradox. He shared with me his theories of how and why God chose to disappear. I guided him through Charlie Manson's interpretations of Beatles lyrics. He explained to me why King Lear was his favorite work in English—because "nothing can be sadder than a hoar head father carrying the body of his daughter."

We *never* discussed the Israeli-Palestinian conflict. It was clearly on our minds. I was a graduate student in International Relations, writing a master's thesis on American policy in the Middle East. Rafik read at least three newspapers every morning, in three different languages. He was the brightest person I knew. And, of course, the conflict affected him every day—walking to work through Jewish neighborhoods, cashing his paycheck using his Jerusalem identity card, writing letters to his jailed relatives, imprisoned for fighting the occupation. But up on his roof, stoned, staring at the starry sky, we stuck to Nietzsche and Bob Dylan. We both sensed that politics would blow up our friendship. Philosophers on the roof, I thought, one unseasonably warm evening in December. Afraid we'll topple off if we collide with the wrong topic.

———

That collision came 15 years later. My aliyah had failed. I moved back to the United States. After two aimless years, I reengaged with my religious self and enrolled in Rabbinical School. Rafik and I exchanged letters for almost a year. I sent books—Scott Turow, Thomas Wolfe, Allegra Goodman, Graham Greene. He wrote long missives about his days mopping floors—no one, I was sure, could

wring so much poetry from housecleaning. But I remained un-
skilled at staying in touch with faraway friends, and anyway my
hotel relationships only reminded me that my dream of living in
Israel had collapsed. Eventually, he stopped writing. When I returned to Jerusalem for my third year of rabbinical school I didn't
look up Rafik. I stayed away from the hotel, crossing the street
and averting my eyes if my path brought me near it. As a budding
rabbi, the idea of visiting Silwan seemed as strange as popping into
Damascus for a day. After that year, my only visits to Israel were as
a rabbi leading congregational trips (we stayed in much less fancy
hotels), or attending conferences. The stoned nights with Rafik on
his Silwan roof seemed like a Borges fiction, surreal adventures
that happened to someone else.

But toward the end of my 30s, I flew to Israel to visit my
mother, who was spending a year in Jerusalem. It was my first time
back alone, no congregants, no colleagues, no wife. My mother
studied during the days, and sometimes evenings, leaving me with
lots of spare time. I took long, nostalgia-bathed walks through my
old haunts—the German Colony, Mt. Scopus, Givat Ram, Bakaa,
Neve Schechter. Former girlfriends lurked in the shadows of my
mind; along with old friends—now olim, new immigrants—from
Brazil, Canada, South Africa, Turkey, and India. After one long
hike, I ducked into my former hotel to use the bathroom. The
thought that Rafik might be in there cleaning the sinks popped
into my head. He wasn't, but the image was enough. The next day
I walked to Silwan.

This was the mid-1990s, between the first and second, dead-
lier Intifada. It wasn't yet physically dangerous for a yarmulke-
clad rabbi/tourist to walk through an Arab neighborhood, but I
did draw some suspicious stares. The boys kicking soccer balls
against the houses could have been the same children I saw 15
years before, same jeans, same t-shirts decorated with 70s band
names—Pink Floyd, Jethro Tull, The Eagles. But time had passed. I
didn't recognize Rafik at first when he opened the door. He looked
taller, though that might have been a change in posture, or a trick
of memory. But he'd grown a thick black moustache, and was

dressed like a men's clothing salesman, blue blazer, black slacks, bright red tie. He knew me right away. "Philip," he said instantly, and I remembered that, apart from one grandmother, he was the only person in the world to call me "Philip." He drew me in for an embrace and I noticed that he even smelled more like an adult, with a lemony cologne or aftershave.

"No fancy meal for you today, my friend," he told me, after he'd sat me down on the familiar scarlet cushions and handed me a hot glass of mint tea. "My mother, she is . . . " He stopped and looked down. "She has passed away."

"Oh, Rafik. I'm so sorry."

"My father, also. Six months later." He looked at me and smiled enigmatically. "But there is good news. I am the owner of this house. And the business."

He filled me in, sharing personal information for the first time in our relationship. After the death of his father, the family catering company went to Rafik and his brother and sister (I didn't know he had a sister). Rafik, however, had no interest in food ("except, you know, for eating"), so his siblings ran the company. Rafik worked at . . . the hotel!

"No!" I said. We laughed. "But Rafik," I said. "You're not . . . "

"Scrubbing toilets? No, my friend. I am now the boss of those who scrub the toilets." He nodded at me. "And you, Philip?"

Am I scrubbing toilets? I thought. But I knew what he meant. He was looking at my baby blue knit kippah, a gift from my wife, and cocking his head in curiosity. During our months scrubbing floors he knew me as a secular Jew from Cleveland who sometimes spent Saturdays with him smoking hashish. I never told him about my religious past, my rabbi father, my many Orthodox relatives. I never told him anything about myself. I took a breath. "I'm a rabbi," I said. "Not," I added quickly, "an Orthodox rabbi. I'm, well, a Conservative rabbi." As if Rafik were well versed in American Judaism's doctrinal differences. As if the distinction mattered in Silwan. But maybe he was. Maybe it did.

He nodded, then flashed the same enigmatic smile, as if he were contemplating a joke I would never understand. "Mazal tov," he said, lifting his glass of tea.

"To you, also."

I was in the middle of telling him the story of how I met my wife when he interrupted me. "Let's take a walk," he said.

I looked at him.

"So sorry to interrupt, Philip. I must go to work. But, first, on the way, a walk. I will show you something."

We turned left at the end of his alley and headed downhill, toward the City of David. The sun was setting over the walls of the Old City, reflecting a golden light across the Hinnom Valley. I felt, as I sometimes did when walking through Jerusalem, that I was strolling through a postcard or a folk tale. But when we reached the bottom, the western border of Silwan, just before the ancient ruins of the archeological park, Rafik put out his hand, like a traffic cop. I stopped. He pointed.

I saw a colorful, hand-painted sign, with Hebrew letters. It said, "Welcome to the Yemenite Village." Rafik signaled to me and we walked to the end of the street. The final three houses on the block looked slightly different than the others. For one thing, they each had mezuzahs on their door posts. And their front doors were decorated with family names, in blue and white Mosaic tiles, the kind you can buy in souvenir shops all over Jerusalem, and especially the Old City.

"Jews?" I said.

He nodded. "Just three. Here in the neighborhood."

I watched the houses, wondering for a moment why Rafik wanted me to see them. But really, I knew why.

"Yemenite Village," Rafik pronounced. "Does it seem to you, Philip, that we are in Yemen?"

I chuckled. Was I supposed to answer?

"Am I now a Yemenite?" Rafik said.

I later discovered that this was the beginning of a Jewish settlement project in Silwan. The Jewish activists buying up houses used the old Hebrew name for the neighborhood, the Yemenite

Village. But at the time, I had no idea what these mezuzahs and mosaics were doing at the bottom of this hill, in this Palestinian neighborhood. But I saw Rafik's face slowly change. His thin lips, the top one now covered with a black moustache, curved downward into a frown. His cheeks turned red. He opened his brown eyes widely and focused them on me. He balled his hands into fists.

"They are moving into Silwan," he said softly, almost a whisper. I turned from his gaze and studied the three houses. Feldman. Greenblatt. Eisen. Not exactly Yemenite names, I thought.

"They don't have other places to live?" Rafik said, talking quickly, his tone shifting, the volume and speed increasing. "There are no other neighborhoods for Jews to settle in Jerusalem?" He looked at me. "You have no other places to live?"

"Whoa," I said. "Rafik, wait a second. I live in Massachusetts. This isn't me. I don't know anything about this."

He stared at me for perhaps another second, maybe shorter. The sun, orange and gold, continued to sink under the Old City walls. Rafik smiled, exhaled. "Of course," he said. "It's just, well you can imagine, can you not? Upsetting."

"Of course."

═══

That night Rafik took me to a fancy restaurant in the German Colony. My old neighborhood had become the East Village of Jerusalem, with funky shops and cute, expensive eateries. Rafik chatted with our young attractive waitress in Hebrew. She laughed when he joked that his parents would be upset to learn he was dating a rabbi. She turned to me and asked if we were really dating. I stumbled through a denial in my suddenly broken Hebrew. Rafik stared at me after the waitress took our order.

"You've forgotten how to speak Hebrew?"

"Well," I said, embarrassed. "I don't live here anymore. So I don't use it."

He shook his head. "This is not right for you, a rabbi. Rusty Hebrew? You should visit more often, Philip. Every year, at least.

And, please, always, come by and see me. Please? Every year. I so value our friendship. Next year, yes? Next year in Silwan."

═══

It wasn't next year in Silwan, but this time we did manage to stay in touch—easier, now that we were both using email. We met for lunch near the hotel at least once every trip I took to Israel. But I never visited his house. I didn't want a repeat of our stroll to the bottom of his neighborhood, and we both realized that Silwan was likely no longer safe for me.

In 2010 I started attending summer sessions at the Shalom Hartman Institute. The program included lunch and evening events, which left less time for Rafik. Or maybe, I thought, this friendship—this relationship—had run its course. Rafik seemed bored and barely comprehending when I described my job as an American pastor. "You are a social worker," he said one time. "We have those. We don't call them clergy." I was even less interested in his work organizing cleaning operations at his now elite hotel. We tried our old trick of discussing books, but Rafik told me he wasn't reading English novels anymore. He'd already mastered the language, so what was the point? I wondered, of course, if we'd hit a conversation dead end because of the elephant in the room—the conflict, the Occupation, Jews in Silwan. Maybe, I thought, that brief moment of rage I saw on his face when he pointed accusingly at the Jewish mezuzahs in the "Yemenite Village" and then turned to interrogate me, was the real Rafik, and we wouldn't resume any intimate friendship until I acknowledged and probed that anger. But my relationship with Rafik was based on my own naïve romantic memories of that sad and beautiful time before my life resolved into coherence, before I figured out what to do with myself. We were two boys on a roof, hashish smoke floating toward the sun, talking Hemmingway and Pink Floyd and Graham Greene, as far from the Israel-Palestine mess than two humans could be who happened to be sitting at the heart of it. I sensed then, and I knew now, that politics would ruin it, even the politics of his own neighborhood.

But one summer, I took a Hartman tour of Jerusalem. The point of these excursions was to introduce us to various viewpoints, from the far left to the far right, so we could hear from everyone, and work through our own syntheses. An oleh from Australia led the tour through the Old City. He focused—in a positive way, he was bragging—on the Jewish project to buy houses in the Arab parts of the city. He confused some of us by referring to a neighborhood he called "the Old Jewish Quarter," where several Jewish families had bought homes. It took me a while to realize he was talking about the Muslim Quarter but using an old Jewish name for the area (that I'd never heard). Later he told us that his organization was also purchasing houses in the Yemenite Village.

"What's the Yemenite Village?" someone asked.

"Silwan," I whispered softly to myself, as our guide pointed across the valley. "By Ir David [City of David]," the guide said. "Those houses on that hill."

"Oh," the man responded. "You mean Silwan."

"Well, we don't call it that. We use the original name, when Jews lived there. We call it the Yemenite Village."

I studied the guide, with his knit kippa, jeans and blue polo shirt. I considered his fluent Anglo-Saxon English, his obvious love for Israel despite the fact that he was born far away. In so many ways, I was like him. He was even roughly my height, my weight, my age. But did Rafik understand that I was fundamentally different than this guy? That I opposed evicting Arabs from their homes? I hated the nefarious plots to purchase the deeds to these houses? That I despised the project of Judaizing Palestinian neighborhoods? That rewriting history by changing the names of Arab neighborhoods was repellent to me, and, frankly, silly?

That night I phoned Rafik. "I want you to know that I understand your anger about Jews moving into Silwan. I do. Really. I'm angry, too."

He paused. "I'm glad, Philip."

"I just don't know what to do about it. What I can do."

He paused again. I pictured him smiling slyly, as he often did, as if he knew more than he was letting on and found it amusing that I hadn't figured it out yet. "I don't know either," he said. "I don't know what you can do about it." I thought I heard the old edge return to his voice. But it disappeared by the second sentence. And maybe I was only imagining it in the first place.

I remembered that rage years later, this past spring, when, during the recent Gaza fighting, The New York Times featured an article about Silwan on its front page. By this time, Rafik and I were only exchanging emails two or three times a year. For health reasons, I stopped working full time, stopped visiting Israel, and was teaching two classes at the local Jewish day school. Rafik was a year away from retiring and poised to leave Silwan, maybe for Haifa, maybe London. The Times article, like many others, traced the Gaza missiles to Jewish attempts to acquire houses in Sheikh Jarrah, another Palestinian neighborhood in East Jerusalem. Unlike other accounts I'd seen those few weeks, this piece noted the similar Judaizing project in Silwan, which had been going on for more than 20 years. Most of the article told the story of a Jewish family somehow acquiring the deed to the ground floor of a four-story home. A Palestinian man had built the building. He lived with his family on the top floors. The Jewish family claimed ownership to the entire house, and was attempting to evict the Arab residents, using Israeli courts. I was astonished to find my eyes filling with tears as I tried to read the article, to follow the tortured legal and moral logic that moved the Jewish family. I gave up reading. All I could think of was Rafik, pointing to the houses, pointing at me, rage just below his surface equanimity, ready to burst. "There are no other neighborhoods for Jews to settle in Jerusalem?" he'd asked. "You have no other places to live?" he'd added, implicating me. Good questions. Among the most important to contemplate, it seems to me, for every Zionist lover of Israel, for anyone seeking to understand our forever war.

The last time I saw Rafik in person was 2014. Another Gaza war had broken out that summer, coinciding with my yearly summer study at the Shalom Hartman Institute in Talbieh, a formerly Arab, now Jewish neighborhood in Jerusalem. Sirens blared that hot July and August whenever missiles flew toward Jerusalem, a call to take cover, in shelters, or, more often, in doorways, or stairwells, or just under some roof, like in an ice cream store, if you're caught, like I was once, at an outdoor concert. On my last day in the country, I had to check out of my Airbnb apartment early in the morning, but my flight didn't leave until late that evening. Normally, I'd have killed the time by walking the streets, soaking in the atmosphere of my favorite city in the world, drinking coffee or beer in outdoor cafes, maybe visit the Kotel. But I wanted to be near shelter in case a Hamas terrorist decided to send a missile my way. I thought of Rafik, and the hotel.

I found him in his office, a corner suite befitting a corporate vice president. His secretary announced me. I laughed when I saw him, with his expensive suit, his silk maroon tie, his shiny brown loafers. "Ever get the urge to clean one of these bathrooms?" I asked. "Every day," he answered. "But I resist temptation." We embraced.

At lunch, we spent an hour discussing the novels of Robert Heinlein, Isaac Asimov and Frank Herbert. I told him the rumor that some famous director was planning a remake of *Dune*. The first one, I told him, was considered among the worst American movies of all time. He laughed. He'd seen the film and kind of liked it. Over coffee and baklava, I asked him about his family, his wife and four children. It seemed like a polite way to wind down the conversation.

"We will leave Silwan," he said.

I nodded. I wasn't surprised. Silwan was a poor, crowded neighborhood. From what I could see, Rafik had prospered. Why not escape the cramped, conflict-ridden ghetto, the malodorous alleys, the dusty kids playing in the street, and live someplace worthy of a man of his means? I myself somehow ended up in La

Jolla, California, a wealthy section of San Diego. I was about to say something along those lines, but he interrupted me.

"Tell me, Philip," he said. "Do you agree with all this?"

"All this?" I asked. That's when I saw him lightly touch his bread knife.

"The killing. The bombing. You know how many Arabs . . . Palestinians have been killed in this Gaza invasion? How many civilians? One thousand."

I nodded. I knew. There would be hundreds more before the next ceasefire, still several weeks in the future. "Rafik," I said. "Of course, it's terrible. Of course, I don't agree." I was about to say something about Israelis also suffering. That four young Jews had been kidnapped and murdered. Or that Hamas shared some of the blame. Fortunately, he interrupted me. At that moment, it wouldn't have been a wise thing to say.

"And Silwan. Silwan. My neighborhood." He gripped his knife. "You've seen it recently? The Jews are now working their way up the hill. More evictions. My cousin. My aunt. Evicted by Jews. You agree with this? This is justice? This is friendship?"

He went on for another 10 minutes, his voice slowly rising, his face shining red against his graying moustache. Radicalized, I thought, as he preached and gesticulated. This is how it happens. He talked about Jews vandalizing a small public park at the bottom of the hill where children play soccer. About loud singing on Friday afternoons, then amplified music on Saturday nights. Rumors of hundreds more families moving in, evicting Arabs. "You have no other places in this country?" he demanded of me. "Nowhere else to go?"

That's when I stopped him. "Wait, Rafik," I said. I held up my hand. He looked at me, then turned his eyes down, embarrassed. "What are you doing here, with me?" I asked. "Are you trying to convince me? Because I'm already convinced. It's a weakness I have. I can always see all sides to an argument, so I end up agreeing with whoever is talking to me. So you've convinced me. You're right, they're wrong. But I'm not the one you've got to convince. I'm going back to San Diego. You live here. You work with Israelis, with Jews every day. This is eating you up. I'm worried about you. Somehow you have to learn to live with this."

He took a breath, looked at me. Exhaled. Smiled, slyly. The red glow of rage faded from his face. All was calm. "Of course," he said. "Of course, you're right." He shook his head. "I look at you now. We were so young when we met. Listen, Philip, your friendship means so much to me. I want to stay friends. Can we leave it at that?"

I nodded. But I said "No. We can't leave it at that. But maybe it's a way to begin."

Chapter Three

The Wise Man of Chelm

For privacy concerns, all the names and some details in this piece have been changed.

I. The Letter

ABOUT A YEAR BEFORE I left Shomrei Torah, I received a letter from Paul Bernstein, our former executive director. He sent it from prison; he was serving an 18-month sentence for stealing over $600,000 from the synagogue. The letter was six pages, tightly spaced, handwritten, blue ink, slightly smudged. He asked for my forgiveness. He wrote that he wasn't sure why he stole, so much for so many years. It was too easy, he wrote. No one was watching him closely. One day he paid for a Disney vacation with a synagogue credit card, made up some story for the accountant, and kept the books away from the volunteer treasurer. He didn't get caught, so he continued—more purchases: gym equipment, airline tickets (business class), furniture. Then—the big stuff. Cash transfers into his account, once a month, or more. It was like an addiction, he wrote. Once he got used to the money, he couldn't stop.

And, he admitted, it was probably ego. He was outsmarting everyone. Our super-successful CEO finance volunteers, our intellectual, highly professional presidents, the talented staff. Me. He began to think that he deserved the money, that he was cleverer, more effective than anyone else. After all, he wrote, he balanced the budget while stealing $100,000 every year.

He wanted me to know that it wasn't personal. The theft, he wrote, was not inspired by our occasional feuds, our turf issues, or really by any bad feeling on his part toward me. The problem, he wrote, was that he lost control of his actions, his raging ego took over, leaving no room for moral reflection. He knows now, he wrote, how wrong he was, how he killed his work relationships, destroyed his family, wrecked his life. He wanted to make amends. Would I forgive him?

The letter carried the whiff of a 12-step communication, the admission that he'd lost control, blaming the ego, the effort to make amends. If I were prone to cynicism, I might have thought his parole was coming up; perhaps he wanted to demonstrate to the authorities that he was working the program. Nevertheless, it was an impressive piece of writing, all six crowded pages. My wife burst into tears when she read it. I asked her if it was because she was suddenly forced to re-live the nightmare time that came in the aftermath of the embezzlement, the six months of non-stop work frenzy that took me away from my family even more than the usual life of a rabbi at a large congregation. She said no, she was simply moved by Paul's sentiments, his contrition, his plainspoken honesty, his losses. She was thinking of his two young girls, who'd played in our backyard and sang sweetly every Tot Shabbat. And his wife, a lovely, shy soul whom everyone liked, and was now left with nothing. She wept for his family.

I took a day to think about it. I decided to forgive him. It wasn't a hard decision. For one thing, forgiveness was one of the central themes of my rabbinate, a topic I'd revisit several times a year, and not just during the High Holidays. For me, the most moving passages in the Torah are when Joseph forgives his brothers, when he rewrites the family's tawdry destiny as a gang of feuding siblings, and claims, "It wasn't you who sent me here, but God." Later he says, "You planned evil for me, but God planned good . . . to save lives . . . I will provide for you and your children." I'd taught congregants that Joseph was able to transcend his justifiable bitterness by conjuring a larger narrative context. Through the great power of the moral creativity, Joseph imagines his ordeal not as a narrowly constructed story about a never-ending family feud, but as God's great plan for the world, to save lives.

If Joseph could do it, why not me? After all, I was doing pretty well. After a year of struggle and chaos, the congregation was growing, and folks credited my leadership. I'd just been offered a senior position at a highly respected international Jewish organization (I took the job). Paul was in jail, broken, defeated, with no conceivable professional future.

I didn't think of it then, but it occurs to me now that it wasn't such a big lift for Joseph to forgive his brothers. He was the richest, most powerful person in the word. Things had gone his way. The brothers were frightened, subservient, pathetic. Why not forgive? The astounding act would have been to forgive while he was still a slave, stuck in a dark pit, beaten, alone. Looking up at them instead of looking down. But that wasn't the case. Anyway, I wrote a letter of forgiveness to Paul. I was conscious that he filled six pages, and I could barely muster one. I threw in some synagogue gossip, some thoughts on how we'd all moved past it. I encouraged him to write back, to contact me when he got out. I mailed it to Paul Bernstein, c/o the Federal Penitentiary.

According to the Talmud, if you renounce bitter revenge toward others, sweetness comes your way. For a while that's how I felt. A new, better job. Health. Loving relationships, friendships. A rich intellectual life. I didn't attribute all of my sudden good fortune to my forgiving Paul, but I felt some pride, and also some peace of mind.

I don't feel that way anymore, for two reasons. One, when I decided to write the letter, I didn't account for the fact that I hated Paul. Truly hated him, in a way that shocked and worried me. I'd never hated anyone, but, Lord, did I hate Paul. And, two, I didn't know that in just a few years, Paul would get a high paying job at a large, important congregation. And I would be sick, and unemployed.

II.Chelm

"Chelm!" Ben Michaels—the associate rabbi at Shomrei Torah, and my close friend and partner for 12 years—would spit out the word, throwing up his hands, whenever synagogue dynamics approached the ridiculous, as they often did during the Paul years. And I'd echo it back. Chelm.

Chelm is the mythical city of Ashkenazi folklore where the people are so foolish they think they can capture the moon by trapping its reflection in a rain barrel, or that they could dispose of all the dirt they unearth in building a synagogue by digging an even larger pit, or that they should place the synagogue tzedakah box out of the reach of thieves, but when they realized then that the rabbi also wouldn't be able to reach it, install a ladder. Chelm, a kind of bizarro version of Vilna, was governed by The Wise Men, who, naturally, were the biggest fools. Ben and I adored these old tales of the The Wise Men of Chelm, until they hit a little too close to home, and became our inside joke. I'd often remind Ben that if Shomrei Torah was Chelm, he and I were The Wise Men.

What made us Chelm? Mostly it was my relationship with Paul, the executive director. The executive director who followed Paul, who bore the biggest brunt in the aftermath of the embezzlement, approached me shortly after she discovered the theft. "One thing I don't understand," she said. "I get why he would steal. People steal, it's a human weakness, and we let him get away with it for so long. But I don't understand why he was an asshole."

Yes, that was the puzzle, the key to understanding our own private Chelm. If he was trying to get away with stealing, why did he work so hard to undermine me, to encourage factions among congregants and the board, to torture staff members who respected me, to draw attention to an obvious power play? After all, I wasn't checking the books. If he wanted to get away with stealing

$100,000 a year (or more), wouldn't he play the good guy, strive to be universally admired, deflect suspicion? Why, then, was he so caustic and unresponsive to at least half the congregation, and so determined to antagonize and undermine me—a rabbi who I have to say, with all modesty, was pretty well liked?

Here are only a few examples.

About a month after he started on the job, he instructed one of our custodians to take down several publicity posters that I had asked him to put up. When the custodian told Paul that it was "the Rabbi" (me) who wanted the posters up, Paul told him never to listen to the rabbi, that the rabbi had no authority to tell him what to do.

The sound system in both the community hall and the main sanctuary was constantly breaking down, with microphones squawking feedback, or not working at all. I asked Paul to look into it. He said he would, but didn't. I asked the custodians to help, but Paul told them not to listen to me. Finally, I brought sound engineers in for a meeting. Paul reluctantly sat in, but never followed through. The sound remained a problem for the rest of his time (the executive director after Paul solved the issue).

The various rooms and halls were invariably set up incorrectly on Shabbat—our busiest 24-hour period, with dinners, bar or bat mitzvahs, baby-namings, a variety of worship experiences, etc... Paul didn't work on Friday nights or Saturdays, so it was left to Ben and me to move tables around, set up directional signs, and convince the custodians, who weren't supposed to listen to us, to help. When I'd complain to Paul, he'd accuse me of disrespecting the custodians and imply that I exhausted everyone with a constant stream of new programming. He'd accuse me of lording it over the staff, and point out that he didn't report to me.

Lording it over the staff. Expecting too much. Acting as if everyone reported to me, that I was the big boss of the congregation. Was he right? Was the issue here an overworked support staff, and an impatient, manic, insensitive egotistical senior rabbi? In the early months of our conflict, I seriously considered the possibility. Paul knew, as did the volunteer leadership, that I'd quarreled with the previous two executive directors. Actually, I'd gotten them fired. I had valid reasons, I thought. But maybe the issue was the inherent conflict—the clashing responsibilities—of a synagogue's senior rabbi and executive director. Or maybe it was me, not knowing my place, not knowing how I presented myself to the staff.

I tried to discuss the issues with Paul, but he would only nod slowly, and I'd sense a silent undercurrent of anger in the way he'd squint and look away. But the fact is, it's hard to say that I was in actual conflict with Paul, since we rarely spoke. I'd hear of his complaints from congregants or other members of the staff. Or he'd assure me that everything was fine, that he'd focus more on the sound system, or the set-ups. But nothing would change. For almost two years, it was simply Chelm. Despite our robust support staff, Ben and I—the rabbis - would show up early on Friday night and Saturday, fiddle with the microphones, *schlep* around books and chairs and tables, put up posters, tape up directional signs, distribute flyers, and hope to finish our chores by the time services started. Then on Sunday I'd email Paul with my list of complaints. Mostly, he wouldn't write back.

After a while, of course, I involved the synagogue president. The last straw had nothing to do with microphones or posters. It was Paul's attempt to fire our pregnant education director. Betty started work at Shomrei Torah at age 19, and she was our longest-serving employee, the only one who predated me. Paul despised her, even though she was close friends with his wife. I didn't know why, but the most logical explanation was that she ignored his instructions. On our organizational chart, Betty reported to Ben, and in any case she was a seasoned Jewish educator, while Paul had no experience at all in the field. In the beginning of his fourth year, when Betty was pregnant with her second child, Paul went around Ben and me, and complained bitterly to board members about Betty. He slammed her clothing choices, her work ethic, accused her of mismanaging her budget. When the president approached me and handed me a memo about Betty, I pointed out that virtually every item was either incorrect or inappropriate. Betty managed her budget correctly—Paul had fudged some numbers. We didn't have a dress code. Her work ethic was excellent, though she'd recently missed more days than usual because of a difficult pregnancy. I'm not a lawyer, I told the president, but wouldn't firing her for being pregnant put us in some legal jeopardy? He backed off quickly.

In general, the volunteers looked at my tension with Paul as the natural outcome of two strong-willed individuals, fighting for power. From their perspective, Paul was their first highly competent, professional executive director; he proved his competence every month with his always balanced (doctored) spreadsheets. At first, I grudgingly accepted that framing. I *was* strong willed, ego driven, and felt strongly that the senior rabbi should be the senior professional of the congregation. But after the Betty incident I encouraged them to re-frame the issue. It's not two well-meaning, hardworking professionals clashing for the sake of heaven. It's right and wrong, I pleaded to individual members of the executive committee. They'd nod, promise to look into it. Or urge me to talk to him, again. The friendlier ones chuckled along with me. Chelm, they repeated—they'd heard the reference from Ben and me. Nothing changed. He'd provoke, ignore, scheme, undermine. Gaslight. Drive me insane with hatred.

But why? Quarrelling with me only drew attention to the details of his work, something he surely would not have wanted. In fact, toward the end of Paul's time at Shomrei Torah, the president told me I would oversee Paul's review process, along with the synagogue treasurer, who grew suspicious at Paul's attempt to fire Betty. This certainly would not have happened if Paul had attempted to placate me, even a little. "Why was he an asshole?" To this day, I don't know. Paul's my enigma, my personal Chelm, without the jokes, the unexplained foolishness that lies at the center of human experience, or at least Jewish institutional experience, or synagogue experience, or at least my experience.

He got caught a few weeks after he resigned abruptly and took a higher-paying job at a larger congregation in DC. Our bookkeeper was preparing for a board report when she noticed an oddity—a $6,000 cash transfer from one of our credit cards to a private bank account. After some quick checking she noticed that the same amount was transferred every month to the same private account. She called the bank; the private account was Paul's. Then she called the new executive director, who called me.

At first, I was sure it was a mistake, or easily explained. Paul was an asshole—but a thief? Our volunteer treasurer, a CPA, spent half a day on our books and confirmed the worst. Not only was Paul helping himself to $6,000 a month, he was using synagogue credit cards to pay for groceries, vacations, gym memberships, luxury travel. We were able to document approximately $600,000, but in all likelihood it was more. We found dozens of payments we couldn't explain, but couldn't attribute directly to Paul.

The next six manic months were the most painfully surreal of my career. It started with two bizarre phone conversations with Paul, where, stuttering and angry, he quickly went from denial, to claiming it had been a mistake, to weepily admitting the theft and begging for mercy because of his children (we all loved his children). We hired communications consultants, lawyers, accountants. We held a packed town-hall meeting with the congregation, where I urged us to stay unified and personally vouched for the remaining staff ("I'd trust them with my life," I boldly asserted).

Oddly, it took some time before Paul was charged. The local police told us they couldn't follow through because Paul now lived out of state, in Washington DC. What a great way to get away with theft, I thought. Smash a window, break into a liquor store, empty the cash register—but then leave town. Ultimately our lawyers and accountants had to gather all the information, present it to the local branch of the FBI, and convince them to investigate. I assumed someone in authority would want to talk to me. And indeed one day two swarthy agents showed up at the front desk and asked if I was available. I was, but I was meeting with Ben (we met every morning, and at least three or four more times every day). Our receptionist told the agents I was in conference, but I'd be available soon. They thanked her politely and left, without leaving a card, or even a message. That was it, as far as law enforcement and me.

In general, the new executive director, the president and I worked well together through the ordeal, but with some painful exceptions. The executive director and the president advocated accountability and house-cleaning. They wanted the entire executive committee to resign. I argued that we couldn't decapitate the lay leadership of our community, plus I wanted to keep the focus on the undisputed wrongdoer—Paul. Yes, the leadership had been negligent, particularly those involved in finance. But Paul had fooled everyone, and now, I felt, was a time for healing and compassion. The new ED and I were good enough friends that we could scream out our disagreement, but it wasn't pleasant. Ultimately the ED and the president decided, over my protest, that the volunteer secretary, who was slotted to be the next president, had to go. That led to the most excruciating conversation of my career. She phoned me one night, hollering, near tears, and demanded to know if I agreed she shouldn't be president. I didn't agree, I told her. She didn't believe me. Wasn't I the boss? But that was the problem, wasn't it? I wasn't the boss. I called the president after speaking with the secretary. By then it was past 11, but she was up (or I woke her). I asked her to reconsider. She, also close to tears, promised to think it over. She did, but didn't change her mind. I called back the secretary, and now we were both in tears. But her were tears of anger. She was raging, Lear-like, furious. At me.

III. Losses

"It's only money." That was a common refrain around the synagogue in the wake of the embezzlement. No one was killed. There was no physical damage, to person or property. The community survived, later thrived. It's still thriving. But there were losses. Gail, the part-time bookkeeper Paul manipulated and lied to everyday, who discovered the theft just weeks after he finally gave her the account passwords, lost her job. Two other staff members had been laid off earlier by Paul, claiming we couldn't afford to keep

them—when the money he stole could easily have paid their sala-
ries. One of those struggled for years before finding another job.
The treasurer lost some measure of community respect, not to
mention the hundreds of volunteer hours he spent unraveling the
mess. Paul's wife lost a husband, and his young children lived with
the stigma of a jailed father.

And there was me. All through the Paul years, I'd been active in fundraising, from the entire congregation, and especially
from our wealthiest members. But I'd been using cooked books in
my presentations, provided by Paul. I doubted our donors would
ever fully trust me again. Then there were those congregational
leaders who supported Paul over me when I complained about his
antics. Or those who stayed neutral, or even those who seemed to
sympathize with me, but did nothing. My public posture was compassion and forgiveness, and I tried hard to internalize a kind of
general amnesty. But, for me, my sermons and stories about moving on were like using Advil to treat a tumor. Roiling resentments
grew slowly inside of me, like a slow-growing cancer. At first, I was
too busy to notice, and too distracted by my own platitudes and
a desperate, contrived self-righteousness. But I couldn't imagine
ever working closely with those leaders again. A former synagogue
president took me aside on the Kol Nidrei night after the theft, just
before services. I wanted to apologize, he said. I'm sorry. You were
right about Paul, and we were wrong. I exhaled slowly. Vindication. For years, during the Chelm era, that's all I'd been looking for.
Someone to tell me, to convince me, that I was right and Paul was
wrong. Such a simple sentence. Of course, I forgive you, I told the
former president. I was anxious to get to the bimah, to look over
my notes, to start the service, to do the job I'd done for almost 30
years. I smiled at him. Is pretending to forgive good enough when
you can't possibly muster true forgiveness? Good question. But it
wasn't the topic of my sermon that night. I'm only contemplating
that now.

Shortly before Paul was to be sentenced, our lawyer (why did
we need a lawyer?) asked me to write a letter to the judge. There
was a possibility that Paul would get off without jail time, he told

me, though that was unlikely. A letter from me could go a long way in ensuring a fair sentence, or at least the sentence recommendation he had worked out with the prosecutors. He also encouraged me to attend the sentencing and read the letter out loud. At first, I balked. Paul's wife would be there, maybe his children. And—jail? Is that really what I wanted for Paul? I opened my laptop, stared at the screen, placed my fingers on the keyboard, and waited to see what might emerge. It wasn't pretty. I filled the page with expletives. Tears streamed down my cheeks, and for the first time in my life (and hopefully the last) I literally trembled with anger. I quickly slapped down the screen, fled my office, and drove to the hospital to visit congregants. Two days later I dashed off a quick note to the judge, emphasizing the three folks who had lost their jobs because of Paul. I told our lawyer I couldn't attend the sentencing because I was too busy with work at the synagogue. There was always work at the synagogue.

Two years later, I got the job offer from that important international Jewish organization. Then Paul's letter from jail arrived. Would I forgive him? I wrote back that I would. But I didn't. I don't.

IV. The Carpet Guy

About a year ago, after I'd left the position at the important international Jewish organization, after a string of poor decisions and bad luck left me facing unemployment, and very shortly after I was struck with the illness that would force me into early retirement, I received a call from a colleague, asking about Paul. He'd seen his resume on LinkedIn. Impressive! He read me the highlights. As executive director of Shomrei Torah, Paul had apparently overseen a massive rebuilding of the synagogue campus. He'd raised $15 million for capital expenses, and $8 million for endowment. Balanced budgets every year. Wasn't that my former synagogue? What did I think of Paul? His *shul* was looking for a new executive director, one with solid experience with budgets and fundraising. Paul seemed perfect. Should they call him, urge him to apply?

My first thought was, practical joke. Distasteful, sure, but sort of funny. But this guy barely knew me; he wouldn't have been aware of how Paul still haunted my nightmares, how I blamed him not only for my professional collapse, but also for the loss of many valued relationships. I groaned softly, chuckled, told him, "Yeah, sure," then waited for the real purpose of the call.

But there was only silence, too long, uncomfortable. Finally, he said, "So, you *do* think we should call him? You'd recommend hiring him?"

I exhaled. I'd been holding my breath. "You're not joking?"

"Joking? Why would I joke?"

"Hold on a second," I said. I turned on my laptop, and called up Paul's resume on LinkedIn. It was open to the public. It was all there. The "highly successful" years at Shomrei Torah. $15 million capital campaign. $8 million endowment. Lies. Lie after lie after lie. For search firms everywhere. For my reading pleasure. I took particular interest in his current position, which, as it happened, was accurate. Director of Catering at Beth Simcha, one of the largest synagogues in the country, and certainly one of the most lucrative Jewish catering operations on the West Coast. I felt my heart racing, the distressingly familiar, bilious, black anger erupting.

"Let me call you back," I said.

———

Almost every Selichot season, I would study the same essay with a group of congregants: "The Carpet Guy" by Ann Lamott. It tells the story of a church volunteer who purchases a used carpet for her Sunday school class, discovers a large mold spot in the middle, and encounters a lying, cheating carpet store owner when she attempts to get her money back. Through numerous phone calls and visits to the store, cajoling and threatening, she waits fruitlessly for the cathartic release of an apology—vindication, not just her money back, but a just resolution. In the end, frustrated, furious, she astonishes the reader by apologizing herself for her behavior. She even buys the guy flowers.

An inspiring story of forgiveness? I would ask. Or offering apologies? Or . . . what? Is Ann a role model for the Jewish process of *teshuvah*? Do we admire her selfless quest for reconciliation and repair?

No! one congregant argued vociferously one year, her eyes bright with an unexpected anger.

"She's a sap?" I suggested. "Naïve?" That was sort of my opinion, though I often find naivete to be an admirable quality.

"No, no. That would be okay. The problem is the Christian nonsense. She thinks the Carpet Guy is Jesus."

"Huh?" I said. I hadn't seen that. But she was right. It's on the first page of the essay. "He [Jesus] is there in the store." I'd thought she meant in the store watching her behavior, but the congregant could be correct. For Ann, Jesus might have been the carpet guy.

"And then," the congregant continued, "she imitates Jesus. She becomes Jesus. Sacrificing herself totally. Buying him flowers, when she did nothing wrong! She takes on his sin, takes on all responsibility, and he doesn't have to do anything. It infuriates me. That's not Judaism. That's not justice, and it's a sham forgiveness. I despise this essay. Why did you make us read it?"

"Huh," I said, again (I was very articulate that evening).

Later, after a few re-readings, I realized that even though the perturbed congregant permanently changed my understanding of the essay, I didn't entirely agree with her interpretation. This isn't a benevolent, loving daughter of God bestowing forgiveness on a poor sinner. There's a darkness to Ann's character that my congregant overlooked. She's contemptuous of the carpet guy from the beginning, a contempt powered by snobbishness. She initially describes the store as a "missing tooth." Then it's "crummy," a "place where bad things go down." The carpet guy himself provokes a rage in Ann that both disturbs and confounds her: He tempts her "into the dark swampy underside of human discourse," opens the "door to the most primitive place inside of me," the anger fuels a malignant energy, "like a drug." She writes him an apology note because otherwise she'd have to murder him. Really, the essay grapples with the question of what to do with a relationship that looms too large in the psyche. What do you do when you hate someone so much you insist that everyone hate him, and it drives you crazy that they don't, that they don't see him like you do, as the absolutely epitome of fraud, dishonesty, injustice? In fact, you want God to hate him every bit as much, if not more, than you do, but you know that's not possible, that to even think such a thought destroys your relationship with the Divine, destroys you. Ann Lamott answers that "you clean up your side the street," before you drown in your own garbage. You write an apology note. You buy the guy flowers. For a few years, Paul was my carpet guy. He brought out the worst in me, not just the anger, but the contempt, the self-righteousness, the ego. Unlike Ann Lamott, when the time came for an honest reckoning, and a sincere exchange of letters, I punted, scribbled out some platitudes. I threw some dirt over the dark rage, and figured I'd go on with my life, with my new job, new relationships. But life has a way of careening off what can seem like the straight path, and buried feelings reemerge. I don't blame Paul for my professional blunders or for the sickness that ended my career. But I do connect his rise to my fall, and connections can blur into blame.

━━

I stared at Paul's LinkedIn resume for an indeterminate amount of time. When you're retired for health reasons, time loses its shape, its crispness, its insistent authority. Let's say it was half an hour. Then I texted the link to the current Shomrei Torah president. I wrote that this was no longer my business—I wasn't an employee of the synagogue. But he might want to note Paul's boast of raising $15 million for the capital campaign, and $8 million for endowment. The true sums for both of those categories was 0 and 0; Paul wasn't involved in either campaign. The only salient accomplishment of his time at Shomrei Torah was his success in stealing over $600,000, until he got caught. I never heard back from the president. A few weeks ago, a current employee told me that Shomrei Torah's executive director asked his counterpart at Beth Simcha how they could have hired Paul, a convicted thief. He responded that Paul had served his time, and that he'd assured them that he'd paid back every penny he'd stolen. "But that's not true, is it?" I asked. "No," he answered, chuckling slightly as if time had rendered the whole incident unfortunate, but now, with retrospective wisdom, also somewhat humorous. "It's not true."

What do I do now? I asked myself. Call the FBI? Write to my congressman? Drive to LA, punch him in the face? Send him flowers? I'm painfully aware that there's an obvious answer. Let it go. Illness bestows the strange gift of utter powerlessness. Unemployment offers similar benefits. I wasn't physically up to challenging Paul's lies, and I wasn't important enough to do anything that mattered. There was nothing I could do, except grumble to a few friends and to my long-suffering family, who all offered the same predictable wise advice.

But letting it go seemed like relinquishing yet another element in my life. I'd already let go of so much: my health, my career, many relationships, several friendships. I thought of the phrase "holding a grudge." At least you're holding on to something. For me, maintaining not merely my judgment of Paul, but my bitter resentments toward him, my anger at how our mutual lives had turned out, meant that I was holding the validity of my work at Shomrei Torah in the palm of my hand, even as so much else slipped away. I was grasping a fading truth—that my career at that particular synagogue at that particular time mattered, that I struggled with Paul, and sometimes lost, but the work, the righteous struggle, made a difference, at least to some people. At least to me.

V. The Wise Man

"Holding a grudge is like taking poison and hoping the other person dies."

A congregant once told me that, and I laughed. "Perfect," I said.

"It's a 12-step saying," she said. "But I think it works for everyone."

"It sounds like a Chelm story," I told her. "The wise man eats and eats, and waits for his enemy to get sick."

But I don't think she'd heard of Chelm.

She quoted me the line the night of our first town hall in the wake of Paul's theft. It was only later that evening that I realized she must have been talking about me. But I'd spoken of reconciliation, of unity, of trusting each other. Where did she hear holding a grudge? The answer, of course is that she sensed it everywhere—in my body language, my facial expressions, the tone of my voice, the way I gripped the podium and cringed every time I mentioned his name. The words said forgiveness, but the music was an operatic call for revenge. Everyone could hear it that night, except for me.

Last month, I ran into several former and present Shomrei Torah colleagues at a bat mitzvah celebration. It was a happy gathering of old friends, swapping stories, laughing, gentle teasing. Lots of talk about moving on, of new careers, new challenges, not to mention new babies and spouses. Inevitably, the topic of Paul came up—the incident had colored many lives besides mine. I mentioned the 12-step line about bitterness and eating poison, and my reinterpretation of the quote as a Chelm story. And here I am, I said. The last Wise Man of Chelm, still eating poison. Well, someone replied. If you were giving a sermon now about holding a grudge, what would you say? I smiled, trying to keep it light. I don't give sermons anymore, I said. All I do now is try to hold on.

Chapter Four

On Hell Planet

MANY YEARS AGO, I got in trouble for teaching *Maus*, the Holocaust graphic novel. Not because of nudity or swear words, the reasons a school board in Tennessee gave for banning the book from its curriculum. At the time of the complaint, I'd read the book at least ten times, and I wouldn't have been able to recall a single naked character, or one instance of salty language. The parents of my student who objected to the book weren't concerned about profanity, or pornographic pictures. They were terrified of how one particular theme might affect their psychologically frail daughter: suicide. And they were right to be concerned. Anyone teaching *Maus* to high school students should approach the novel's suicides with care and sensitivity. These disturbing self-annihilations haunt the novel, and they've haunted me, and probably anyone who's actually read and engaged with Art Spiegelman's strange masterpiece.

Two suicides are central to the narrative. The first occurs in the terrifying "Prisoner on the Hell Planet" section, a separate graphic piece Spiegelman published many years before *Maus*, and then later inserted into the novel. The short, 4-page, black and white sequence—the only part of the story which features real human beings and not animals - portrays the suicide of Art's mother and its aftermath. Art's father Vladek, Maus' chief narrator, finds his wife, Art's mother, dead in a bathtub. Spiegelman draws himself here in a striped jail uniform, a prisoner not merely of his grief, but his maddening guilt, when friends and family imply that he was responsible for his mother's death. A cousin scolds him, saying "Now you cry! Better you cried when your mother was still alive!" In the final panels, we see Art in a single cramped jail cell surrounded by an endless warren of barred cells screaming "You murdered me Mommy, and you left me here to take the rap." The artwork for "Hell Planet" is as creepy, grotesque, and as nightmarish as the Auschwitz body piles in the later sections of *Maus*. The psychiatrist who informs Art of his mother's suicide becomes a demonic, cackling skeleton. Gigantic coffins take over 4 separate panels. Spiegelman's subconscious thoughts—"MENOPAUSAL DEPRESSION. HITLER DID IT! MOMMY! BITCH - swirl through a panel depicting Art's mother lying in a bathtub filled with blood. Ironically, the only subtlety in the section is also the one actual instance of nudity in the novel. Art drew his mother naked in the bathtub. But you have to study the images closely to notice the nude breasts. The other grotesqueries overshadow it. In 25 years of reading the book, I never spotted Anja Spiegelman's naked body until I read the Tennessee School Board's complaint.

Anja's suicide is important to the novel because Anja's story is the great unresolved tension in the book, the issue that perpetually divides Art and his father. Art interviews his Holocaust survivor father throughout the novel, but he also yearns to tell his dead mother's story. He discovers that Anja kept a diary, and he becomes obsessed—"I have to find that diary." When, at the end of Volume One, his father admits that he burned all his mother's papers, Art explodes, clenches his fist, and seems ready to punch his father. He quickly calms down, but the last word in the volume, the first published edition of *Maus*, is Art mumbling that his father is a "murderer"—in other words that he murdered his mother by burning her diary. Why exactly did Anja kill herself a full 25 years after liberation? How did she experience the horrors that her husband Vladek Spiegelman described? We'll never know, and that ignorance prevents any real reconciliation between father and son, and any remotely satisfying resolution in the novel.

The second suicide—possibly as important - is really a murder suicide. Spiegelman depicts it just a few pages after the "Prisoner on the Hell Planet" sequence. In Vladek's telling, he and Anja send Richieu their five-year-old child, to a "safer" ghetto, to live with relatives. When the Nazis are poised to liquidate that ghetto, Richieu's aunt Tosha feeds the child and another cousin poison, and then kills herself. We can only imagine how this murdered martyred brother haunted Art's childhood—a brother he never met. We know for sure that Richieu's mini-Masada narrative loomed large for Art, because he dedicated the second volume of Maus to him, and included a real-life, non-animal photo of the boy on the dedication page.

The suicides form a lens which allow us to see other characters more sharply. For much of the book, Vladek is insufferable. He spooks the young Art with Holocaust horror stories. He nags and irritates his adult son over a host of minor issues—his coat, eating, a piece of wire. He plagues his second wife Mala with a never-ending stream of complaints. But he's undeniably a survivor. He pedals on his exercise bike while Art smokes. He walks every day. During the worst of the Holocaust—homeless on Poland's winter streets, or inhaling Auschwitz's chimneys, he finds creative ways to survive. He's the one who *didn't* kill himself and with that bare fact he redeems himself and commands our sympathy. Similarly, Art is the brother who was *not* the victim of a murder suicide. His life becomes painfully complicated because of his Holocaust survivor parents, but he's never put in his brother Richieu's position. Art, like Harry Potter, like his father, is the boy who lived.

=====

It was the day after we read Richieu's story that my student Ellen's (not her real name) mother phoned me. She didn't want to meet at my office in the synagogue because she didn't want anyone to know she was seeking out a rabbi, her daughter confirmation teacher. So we met at Starbucks. She told me about her daughter's anxiety disorder. How tied up it seemed to be with chronic depression.

She'd never tried suicide, but she'd thought about it, and discussed it openly, terrorizing her parents. I ignored my steaming latte listening to Ellen's Mom. My first response was okay, no problem, we'll skip *Maus*. I'll find something happy to read, maybe Moshe Waldoks *Big Book of Jewish Humor*. Or we'll watch Mel Brooks movies. The idea of the class was to engage the students with Jewish ideas and identity, not depress them.

But Ellen's mother said no. Unlike the school board in Tennessee, she didn't want to remove the book from my curriculum. It's important, she said, to teach young Jews about the Holocaust. Several of her relatives were victims or survivors. Understanding what happened "over there" is an essential element of Jewish identity, she said, ignoring her tall black coffee. And you can't teach the Holocaust honestly without bumping up against uncomfortable feelings—sadness, fear, rage, despair. Teach the book, she urged me. But don't skip over the suicide scenes. Talk about them. Analyze what brings people to that level of desperation. Ellen, she said, needs to talk openly about her struggles. At least that's what her therapist was recommending. And, in any case, she said, we can't control what books Ellen reads in school, or at synagogue, or on her own. But if she's going to encounter suicide in literature, better it be with a rabbi and sympathetic peers who can discuss the subject with wisdom and compassion.

I didn't necessarily agree that knowing the Holocaust constituted an "essential" element in Jewish identity. I'd chosen *Maus* for that confirmation class because I thought it was a book of sly genius, and that teens would enjoy learning Jewish history from a comic book. But I did agree that if we were going to teach the Holocaust—and we were, we do—then we couldn't elide unpleasantness. No trigger warnings could salve Babi Yar's murder pits or Treblinka's gas chambers or the massacres at the Warsaw ghetto.

Or suicide. Suicide is a not so hidden theme of Holocaust history and literature. Many members of the Jewish councils whose job it was to provide lists of Jews for deportation killed themselves, including Warsaw's Adam Czerniakow and Vilna's Jacob Genz. The suicide rates were high in the death camps. And what was the Warsaw Ghetto rebellion if not a mass suicide mission? And, perhaps most hauntingly for those who study Holocaust literature, several Holocaust writers died by suicide. Thane Rosenbaum noticed this and crafted a novel—*The Golems of Gotham* - featuring the ghosts of Primo Levi, Jerzy Kosinski, Paul Celan, Jean Amery, Piotr Rawicz, and Thadeus Borowski, all of whom survived the Shoah, wrote about their experiences, and then killed themselves years after liberation.

The phenomenon of the suicide writer suggests there's a kind of long Covid affect to the Holocaust, especially if you immerse yourself deeply into it. Thirty years later, the fumes linger, can still murder you, or induce you to murder yourself. This is all grim stuff, but Rosenbaum, handles the material with surprising humor and grace. In *Golems of Gotham*, the revived writers comically transform Manhattan into a kind of anti-Holocaust theme park. Showers stop working. Tattoo parlors disappear. Striped clothing is outlawed. Even the New York Yankee pinstripes vanish, irritating short stop Derek Jeter.

And there's an unexpected happy ending. The first paragraph of the book describes a shocking suicide. A Holocaust survivor—protagonist Oliver Levin's father—shoots himself while performing an aliyah in the synagogue on Shabbat. He spills blood and brains on the Torah. Seconds later his wife, Oliver's mother, also a survivor, swallows a cyanide pill. Naturally, these suicides haunt Oliver, who's already traumatized by a childhood listening to his parents' tales of horror. He clings to normalcy enough to marry and father a child. But divorce and a writer's block push him into a suicidal depression. His daughter Ariel, seeking to rescue her father, performs a kabbalistic séance, summoning the spirits of Oliver's parents, who drag along the suicide writers. The book is funny, but darkly cynical, sometimes verging on the nihilistic, especially in the character of Rabbi Vered, yet another survivor, who dedicates his life to denouncing God and religion, and later also kills himself. Until the last page, it seems possible, even likely, that Oliver will join his parents in suicide. But he doesn't. Ariel's spell works. The suicide ghosts turn out to be good fairies, spreading life instead of death. Oliver, in contrast to his parents, but very much like Vladek and Art, emerges as another boy who lived.

While discussing the suicides in *Maus*, I read Ellen's confirmation class passages from *The Golems of Gotham*. I wanted to contextualize the suicides, demonstrate that it was possible to transcend the heavy weight of history, inject some measure of hope and light into this smoky subject, show that both *Maus* and *The Golems of Gotham* teach the possibility and importance of choosing life. Even though I wasn't at all sure that was the point of either novel. I just thought it would help to throw a few laughs into the mix. And I wanted to reach Ellen.

Years later I asked her if I succeeded. We'd gotten back in touch during the pandemic when she found me on Facebook. She was getting married, and she wondered if I would perform the wedding—an informal ceremony, masked, in her parent's backyard. I was delighted with the news and the request, and for weeks we traded Facebook notes on our lives. Since I was getting ready to teach *Maus* again, this time to a high school class at a Jewish day school, I asked her what she remembered about her confirmation class. "Not much," she replied. "Those were horrible years. Honestly, I don't think I paid much attention in class. I was only attending because my parents made me. I do remember that you were very kind to me. That I remember."

Huh, I thought. I'd pretty much designed the curriculum for her, but she didn't notice. I asked her if the class, or even just the book *Maus*, affected her thoughts about suicide. It took her several days to respond. "It's funny," she wrote. "I don't remember being suicidal at all. I asked my parents, and they back you up, I guess I had threatened it, but I don't remember doing so. I was probably making it up. Or I've blocked it out. But, honestly, even if I was genuinely suicidal, I don't think a single class or book would have made a difference. But I don't remember a lot from those times. Maybe you helped. Who knows?"

Indeed, who knows? I dropped the subject from our correspondence. But I was still attentive on the subject of suicide when I taught the class. I warned the parents, asked for their feedback.

As Ellen's mother had urged all those years ago, I lingered over the Hell Planet and Richeau sections of the book, leaving plenty of time for class discussion and engagement through assignments. When the news broke about the Tennessee School Board, I could only chuckle sadly. They're concerned about nudity and swear words, and I'm up at night worrying about the suicides.

As it happened, the same semester I taught *Mous*, I also taught a course which dealt with the prototypical Jewish mass suicide story: Masada. I recalled that we use to teach the story as heroic defiance. But now, Jewish educators are encouraged to interrogate the story, suggest alternatives, point out that the very agency the Masada victims employed in slaughtering each other could have been used for other choices. That semester, I also thought about the suicides in my family, my sister-in-law, mother-in-law, and the suicide note I found written by my mother - she never followed through with it, and we never talked about it. I'm besieged by suicide, I thought. But there's no point in burying the subject, or engaging in denial. In our frighteningly connected, meta world, a world where teen anxiety has become epidemic, young people know all about suicide. It's a terrible topic, but one we can't ignore. And, I believe, it's a key to understanding the Shoah, and the lessons we derive from it, particularly for this generation who will grow up never having met a survivor. If we're going to teach the Holocaust—and we are—we of course must allow for nudity and profanity, but those aren't the problem. The problem—one of the problems, at least—is suicide. Even so, we'll teach it.

I couldn't perform Ellen's wedding ceremony. It would have involved travel, and, during those acute pandemic times, I wasn't ready for that. But she posted photos from her parents' springtime garden. With its red and white roses, thick, deep, green grass, and leafy oak trees, it was bursting with life. Under a virginal white huppah, a handsome groom, young and filled with energy, wrapped in a brand-new tallit, lifted the white veil from his glowing bride. Look at them, I thought to myself, a tear escaping from one of my eyes. Look at this young Jewish couple. Look at my former sad student, this rejoicing bride with the widest smile I'd ever seen. Look at her now. The woman who lived.

Chapter Five

Notes from the Narrow Place

Fieldtrip

LAST NOVEMBER, ROUGHLY NINE months into the pandemic, I was talking to my high school Jewish Philosophy class about seals. Half the students stared at me through computer screens—or I should say, they stared at their screens; I have no idea what they were actually looking at. The other half, those present and in person, wore masks, which effectively hid their boredom (or fascination or disgust), and muffled their voices. My double mask muffled my voice, and vapors from my breath fogged up my glasses. I was using a local dispute over a seal incursion at La Jolla Cove to illustrate the tension between humans and nature. Normally, I told the students, we'd take a fieldtrip to the beach, watch the seals, talk to the people swimming with them, and to the protestors urging humans to stay away. Maybe wade into the water ourselves. But this year, I said, of course that's out of the question. Instead we'll . . .

———

Massive whining ensued, howls of protest, slamming of books, tossing of pens. Not so unusual for teenagers, even high school seniors. But even through my fogged-up lenses, even through their muted screens, their reactions seemed exaggerated. It wasn't as if these coastal San Diego students had been denied trips to the beach in their lives. "We can never do anything," one outraged Yale-bound young man complained, holding on to his mask, so it wouldn't slip off his nose. "Everywhere is off limits. Everything!" He sounded like a spoiled 5-year-old, but I nodded. I got it. I agreed. The canceled La Jolla beach fieldtrip was a kind of microcosm of their pandemic year. Beyond the fear, and the illness, and the unspeakable losses, there was the sheer wall of limits, the narrowing of experience, the constriction of possibilities, of choice that defined this year for them and for all of us. All those things we could no longer do: visit friends, shake hands, eat at restaurants, play basketball, touch, hug, flirt, skip school and head to Coachella, stand close to a teacher while she explains something, lighten up a boring class with a fieldtrip. Narrowness defined the pandemic for all of us, but somehow I felt it was worse for high school kids. Their immediate pre-Covid lives were characterized more by possibilities than reality. A high school senior spends a year on the cusp, a year contemplating new potential, new personas, new horizons. Bursting free defines their sensibilities. Where will I go? they wonder constantly, allowing themselves to dream more than they ever will in their lives. Who will I be? Their reality shifted in one week in March from a life suffused with potential to one defined by what they could not do.

The Narrow Place

A single line from Psalms went through my mind as I was disappointing my class of sad teens: *Min ha'meitzar karati yah anani b'merchav yah.* "Out of the narrow place, I call to God. God answers me from the expanses." We're all in the narrow place, I thought, yearning for the expanses. That night I looked up the psalm—it's 118, verse 5—and discovered some commentary that eventually shifted my own theology, the way I think about God from my own experiences and my own particular circumstances. Two medieval commentaries—Radak and Ibn Ezra—point out that the word for God in the line—"Yah"—is made up of exactly half the letters of

God's full name (YHWH). It's as if when I'm stuck in the narrow place, I only have access to half of God. The constriction in my possibilities includes my spiritual potential. It's cut off. Halved.

But the psalmist also uses the word "Yah" in the second half of the verse, where God answers from the *merchav*, the wide place, the place of expansion. The message seems to be that I can find as much of God in the narrowest of places, stricken with the worst physical and spiritual paralysis, as I can in the land of freedom and possibility. "Half of God is enough for the world," Radak writes. The point is that no matter how constricted your life, how narrow the prison cell, how debilitating your disease, spiritual resources glimmer from the walls of the jailhouse, available, sufficient, and possibly healing. When it comes to God's help in the narrow place, the trick is not seeing the glass as half full. It's finding the fullness in what's really half empty.

The Hebrew word I've been translating as "narrow place" is *meitzar*. The root word is *tsar*, meaning "narrow," and it's sometimes translated as "distress," or "sorrow." But just a glance at the letters shows that it's linguistically related to the word *Mitzrayim*, Hebrew for "Egypt." Being in the narrow place is to be thrust back to Egypt, enslaved, confined. But, of course, redemption *begins* in Egypt. Another line from a different psalm (91:15) serves as a kind of response to our call to God from our own private slavery. In a rare case of speaking in God's own voice, the psalmist writes, "When he [a stricken individual] calls to me, I will answer him. I am with him in his narrowness (*tsarah*). I will rescue him." The prisoner thinks she's calling out to God from behind her prison walls, with her praying flying outwards to Heaven. God responds no, I'm with you *in Egypt*. Even if I'm only half there, even if I'm barely discernable, I still glimmer toward potential, toward some kind of freedom. I'm not coming to rescue you. I'm already there. The wide places you yearn for are hidden in your prison cell. We'll find them together. You just have to work with me, trust that, together, you and I will discover hidden sources of expansiveness. Trust. And wait.

Easier said than done.

Lungs

July, 2019.

Here are some of the things I can no longer do:
Bike.
Play tennis.
Snorkle.
Run.
Eat much of what I enjoy.
Teach.
Work.
Socialize.
Sleep through the night (and often sleep at all).
Breathe, with full confidence.

Asthma is a disease which, among other things, and for mysterious reasons, constricts the lungs. The bronchial tubes narrow, making it harder to breathe. I've suffered with asthma for most of my life. When doctors ask me when it started, I tell them I can't remember; it's always been with me. But for more than 50 years, it was episodic, and fairly well managed through medications. But somehow at age 58, the inhalers and pills stopped working. Anyone who's dealt with a debilitating chronic illness, a high percentage of the U.S. population, knows what happened next. A year of poking, prodding, tests, tubes through the mouth, through the nose, diets, specialists, drug trials, experimental treatments, IV lines, injections, exhausting flights to consult with additional specialists, tears, despair, alternatives, supplements, restrictions, scoldings, encouragement. Tens of thousands of dollars. Insurance battles, baffling bills. Kind doctors, indifferent doctors, wise doctors, nasty bastard doctors. And no improvement. I remained in my own private Egypt, with constricted lungs, restricted activity and a narrowing life.

I'm a rabbi, so it might be logical to guess that I called out to God from my narrow place. In fact, like many rabbis I suspect, I dove headfirst into modern, Western biotechnological remedies:

pharmaceuticals, CT scans, spirometry, bronchoscopy, FeNO analysis, ph monitoring, echocardiogram. With no regrets. I'd do it again, even though it all came to almost nothing. I put my God side on hold, as if it were a hobby that I'd get back to once the serious stuff was taken care of. It wasn't until a speech pathologist (long story) recommended I try meditation and breathing exercises that my spiritual muscle reemerged. At first it was just a memory of a rabbinical school professor teaching us that God's full name (YHWH) sounds like an exhale, like breath—especially the first syllable, Yah. And the breathing exercises, controlled inhalation and exhalation, worked, sort of. They didn't cure me, but they provided some fractional relief, and when it comes to breathing, any relief is monumentally significant. Of course, it wasn't a cure in the medical sense, because I wasn't adding anything to my body. I was working with the diseased lungs I had. It turned out I could find some healing—a kind of minor redemption—within my own troubled breath. With half a breath. Half of God was still there. Yah. I didn't need to call out into the ether from my narrow place. God, a fuller exhale, deeper breaths, was already there.

Or, in non-theological terms, I learned to live with it. When I discovered I could do more with my diseased lungs with the breath already at hand, I slowly expanded my activities. I started walking with a friend. When he noticed my relatively non-infirm pace, he wondered if I could run. A little. I tried. It didn't seem to damage me physically, and psychologically it made a huge difference. I ran/walked almost every day for a year.

Every once in a while, I'd glance at my bike, shoved into a corner of the garage. Two months before my fateful asthma attack, I skidded into a rut on the Mission Beach bike bath. I tumbled off the bike, scraped my forehead on the tar, and broke my wrist. After returning home from the emergency room, my wife stored the blood-stained 21-speed bicycle in the garage. For two months I considered repairing it, but chickened out. Then I got sick, and then the pandemic, and bike shops became unavailable. I dreamt of riding. But still I was running. Moving, almost every day.

The next logical step was work. I'd retired early because my life had narrowed to a series of doctors' appointments, tests, and treatments, all in a fog of fatigue and despair. It wasn't just the psychological stress of juggling work and medicine, it was the bone-wearying fatigue of keeping it all straight, the professional and the personal: finding substitutes, wrestling insurance forms into coherence, researching treatments, planning pre-school Shabbat dinners, breathlessly leading middle school Israel programs. Altogether, it was too much, so I quit.

But I had something left. At least half a breath. Yah. So after a year of early retirement, I asked the school where I'd worked if there was a part-time teaching position available. I was fortunate; there was. In some ways, it was a letdown. I'd been a decision maker at the school, part of the leadership team, and for the past few decades of my career, I'd either been in charge of an institution, or near the top. Now I was just teaching (just!) and, as a part time teacher, well out of the circle of decision makers. But it didn't take long, nor was it a particularly inspired insight, before I discovered that the spiritual expansiveness of a moment teaching a child—face to face, even through a screen, even through a mask—matches a lifetime of satisfaction and frustration directing a large institution. I was still in Egypt, too tired for full-time work, to breathless to resume anywhere near my previous level of physical activity. But I'd found width within my narrowed circumstance. I have a name for that previously hidden expansiveness. I call it Yah.

The Narrow Bridge, This Sweet Old World

Shortly after I retired, my sister-in-law took her own life. Carol was one of the most expansive people I knew. A brilliant storyteller and lawyer, when she held forth on her latest absurd, fascinating case, always a unique study in human frailty and nerve, waving her hands, pointing her thin fingers, winking, smiling slyly, people gathered round, like planets in orbit. The one time I consulted her on a legal case, she spent over two hours with me on the phone, walking me through various choices and scenarios. The next day she sent me a 3,000-word, tightly argued, yet somehow breezy and funny memo with my options.

She spent wildly on gifts. She gave away thousands of dollars to people she barely knew. When I first met her, she played piano so skillfully, and sang so beautifully, I was sure she was going to pursue a career in music. She played college tennis. I'd played my whole life; she beat me easily. She read voraciously. She was tall, thin, beautiful, talented, funny, intelligent, hugely successful. Strangers fell for her. She killed herself.

How did her full life narrow to a single dark, dense point, a point where, at least for her, she was left with literally only one choice? It's a mystery. The only answer—baffling, unsatisfying— was mental illness. When I spoke at her funeral, I avoided all talk of mental illness, didn't mention the suicide. I spoke about her generosity, her startling capacity to widen her circle of empathy, her glimmering charisma. I didn't touch on the darkness that overwhelmed her. I didn't want to diminish the glow I was conjuring, even for myself, and anyway I had very little to say about it. But as I gathered my memories and considered where illness had led Carol—to her final destination, the place where we'll all end up—I felt a dull ache of familiarity. Limits. Constriction. Options and activities, choices and opportunities that formerly defined me, gradually cut off. One by one. I wasn't suicidal. But I think I knew what it felt to have the walls close in. To look around at what's left of your life and discover that you're back in Egypt.

When I got home, I put on a song by Lucinda Williams called "Sweet Old World" about a friend who'd taken his life. "Look what you lost when you left this world," the narrator sings. "Breath from you own lips. The touch of fingertips." She continues with a litany of missed experiences. "The sound of a midnight train. Wearing someone's ring. Someone calling your name . . . this sweet old world." Quotidian. Ordinary. Common. Yet each one a moment of infinite potential, of expansiveness. I had my own litany. Yah was with me, here in Egypt, when I twirled my golden wedding ring around my finger, when it reflected the sunlight off its smooth surface into my eyes. When I could hear my own breath, sometimes labored but always steady, always forming the word Yah. When my fingers touched someone else's, or even when I caught the sad eyes of a loved one on a computer screen, wondering when we'd see each other again.

"The whole world is a narrow bridge," Rav Nahman, tuberculosis sufferer, taught us. I imagine his breathing came harder than mine, and I certainly have better access to medical care, and a less serious illness. Yet he bequeathed to us an exquisite universe of teachings, wisdom that now expands through space and time. If the whole world really is a very narrow bridge, it means that we're all stuck in the narrow place. We're all back in Egypt. This was certainly true this past pandemic year, when even a two-hour seal-gazing fieldtrip to the beach with a bunch of restless, yearning teenagers was out of the question. We survived, those of us who did, by finding grace through Zoom, turning computer screens into open portals, widening the range of spirit and activity, while stuck at home. We also took masked walks and took note of the sweet things in this narrow, old world. Grass, sky, sun, pets, rain. As Radak would say, we made do with half of God, with Yah. It was just enough.

In late February, I got my first shot. I celebrated by hauling my bloody, dusty bicycle to a repair shot. Amazingly, the bike endured less damage than I. It was fixed a day later, but I waited. In mid-March, I got my second shot at a Rite Aid pharmacy, not far from my house. Assuming I'd be sick the next day (I was, and for the next two days), I tentatively approached the newly gleaming, good-as-new bike. I hadn't ridden in over two years, since the accident. I held my breath and wheeled the great machine into my driveway. I twisted my thigh a bit—a pain that would last a week— but I mounted the bicycle. There's a steep downhill incline right outside my house, so I glided a few feet then peddled easily. Wind hit my face. It was a cool day for Southern California. I noticed a young girl I'd never seen riding a tiny white bike, grinning at the breeze, her hair flying through her helmet. A tall neighbor whose name I didn't know waved at me. I saw bushes and workmen and houses and trees. Breath flowed into my body, and out. I felt freer than I had in years.

Of course, this was all downhill. At the bottom would come exertions, decisions, gravity, limitations. But that was for later. For now, for this blessed moment, I was riding free, taking in the sights, wallowing in the sublime awful beauty of this narrow bridge, this sweet old world.

Chapter Six

Crowns

Rab Judah said in the name of Rab, When Moses ascended on high he found the Holy One, blessed be He, engaged in affixing coronets to the letters.

Said Moses, Lord of the Universe, Who delays you?

He answered, There will arise a man, at the end of many generations, Akiva b. Joseph by name, who will expound upon each tittle heaps and heaps of laws. Lord of the Universe, said Moses; permit me to see him. He replied, Turn thee round.

Moses went and sat down behind eight rows [and listened to the discourses upon the law]. Not being able to follow their arguments he was ill at ease, but when they came to a certain subject and the disciples said to the master Whence do you know it? and the latter replied It is a law given unto Moses at Sinai he was comforted.

Thereupon he returned to the Holy One, blessed be He, and said, Lord of the Universe, Thou hast such a man and Thou givest the Torah by me! He replied, Be silent, for such is My decree.

Then said Moses, Lord of the Universe, Thou hast shown me his Torah, show me his reward. Turn thee round, said He; and

Moses turned round and saw them weighing out his flesh at the market-stalls. Lord of the Universe, cried Moses, such Torah, and such a reward! He replied, Be silent, for such is My decree.

-TALMUD, MENAHOT

WHAT DID RABBI AKIVA believe? It's an important question because, according to many rabbinic sources, the Romans tortured him to death for his beliefs. Yet, in the Talmud and the Midrash, Akiva says very little about God. In fact, these sources contain almost no systemic theology. The best we can do is infer Akiva's faith system from a handful of stories, particularly the one above, where God is drawing decorations on the letters of the Torah, and Moses wonders why. By comparing Moses and Akiva in this strange and beautiful tale, we can extrapolate a surprisingly useful post-modern theology that flows through Judaism's sacred texts.

In the story, Moses has climbed Mt. Sinai to receive the Torah and bring it to his recently liberated people. When he sees God adorning the letters, his first concern is timing. What's the delay? he asks. From Moses' perspective, the Israelites need the law right now. Readers of the story, familiar with the Biblical text, understand that the people are about to reject Moses and turn to the Golden Calf. Moses senses or intuits the coming anarchy. He doesn't have a moment to spare. The people need order, structure, commandments. But God's wasting time, drawing crowns.

Moses here exhibits a *pshat* personality; he's only interested in the literal meaning of the Torah's words. For Moses, the Torah is a tool he needs to build social cohesion, like a constitution. He's got a job to do, and he'll do it with the *pshat,* with the literal meaning. It wouldn't occur to the Moses in our story to dig deeply for hidden meanings, to somehow discover "heaps and heaps" of laws buried in a decoration. There's no time for creative reflection, and really, it's not necessary. The people, right now, need to learn right and wrong, to honor their parents, to avoid theft, to worship the one God. Why dive past the surface if the surface is all you need?

Akiva, on the other hand, leaves the *pshat* far behind. He teaches a Torah that Moses—the first reader—doesn't recognize. But when his students wonder where Akiva got all this, he tells them it came to Moses at Sinai. Akiva's majestic creativity, in other words, comes strictly through interpretation. He's not writing a new Torah. He's ceaselessly discovering new meanings in the old one. Akiva here exhibits a *drash* personality—a method of Torah study where you open your mind to the possibility of infinite interpretations. In the story, Akiva invents Torah study as a spiritual activity. He encounters God's infinite presence in the letters of the Torah, and in their decorations. God, for Akiva, means endless possibilities, bottomless interpretive opportunities. If Moses himself doesn't recognize Akiva's Torah, then Torah can go anywhere, mean anything. To believe in God is to believe in the infinite power of the text, along with the human individual's spiritual will to interpret, to ask questions, find new meanings. No line of inquiry is ever closed off because everything is possible. "Turn it and turn it," as it says in Pirkei Avot. "Everything is in it."

Ironic then, that our story ends with God twice closing off any further questions from Moses. The first time, Moses modestly wonders why God chose him and not Akiva to receive the original Torah. God tells him to shut up. God takes no questions on the subject. The second time, a horrified Moses questions how Akiva could meet such a gruesome end. God again shuts him up. A story which teaches and glorifies limitless inquiry, infinite interpretive possibilities, ends with God imposing limits.

But the limits are for Moses, a man of the *pshat*, a leader and hero stuck at the surface. God doesn't shut up Akiva. In fact, we know from a different story that Akiva, the hero of *drash*, never gives up searching for, and finding new answers.

> The Sages taught: Four entered the Pardes [Orchard] and they are as follows: Ben Azzai; and ben Zoma; *Aḥer* and Rabbi Akiva. Rabbi Akiva, said to them: When you reach pure marble stones, do not say: Water, water, because it is

stated: "He who speaks falsehood shall not be established before My eyes" (Psalms 101:7).

Ben Azzai glimpsed and died. And with regard to him the verse states: "Precious in the eyes of the Lord is the death of His pious ones" (Psalms 116:15). Ben Zoma glimpsed and was harmed, i.e., he lost his mind. And with regard to him the verse states: "Have you found honey? Eat as much as is sufficient for you, lest you become full from it and vomit it" (Proverbs 25:16). Aḥer chopped down the shoots of saplings. In other words, he became a heretic. Rabbi Akiva came out safely.

-Talmud, Hagigah

How did Akiva "come out safely?" Many commentaries have struggled with this question. The first clue comes from the only bit of dialogue in the story. Akiva warns against saying "Water water," because it might be a "falsehood." Akiva here seems to be cautioning his colleagues not to get stuck in surface conclusions. Just because something looks like water doesn't mean that's what is. Akiva's gift for interpretation, for transcending the pshat, saves his life.

But a fuller theology emerges from the deeper question: what is the Pardes? Rashi and many others suggest it's mystical or philosophical contemplation, but Eli Wiesel, in his book *Sages and Dreamers*, offers the most interesting, and ultimately the most useful interpretation. He suggests the four friends are contemplating the problem of evil, why an all-powerful benevolent God would allow the innocent to suffer. He points out that each of the four would have lived through the destruction of the second Temple, their Holocaust. They would have personally witnessed the loss of sovereignty, the slaughter of thousands and the collapse of their theological system. How do we reconcile Israel's defeat, children dying, a city destroyed, with a caring, all-powerful God, who chooses Israel, and whose Presence yearns for Jerusalem? From a pshat perspective you can't. That stark reality—that God doesn't care or can't intervene - is too much for Ben Azzai and Ben Zoma; one dies, the other goes insane. Aher, the other, Elisha Ben Abuyah, embraces the cold theological logic of the disaster and becomes a heretic. Only Akiva survives as a committed Jew because he reads beyond the pshat. Using the creative powers of drash, he discovers a deeper, hidden truth both in reality and in the text—that there's a world to come, a place where God rewards the righteous fully, and punishes the wicked. The bitter logic of pshat destroys Ben Zoma and Ben Azzai, and expels Elisha. Drash rescues Akiva, and therefore Judaism.

Another story validates Akiva's theology of reading. Elisha Ben Abuya, Akiva's Pardes companion, sees a young boy follow his father's instructions by climbing a tree, sending away the mother bird, then collecting the eggs. In these actions, the boy fulfills the only two commandments—honoring his parents, and sending away the mother bird—where the Torah explicitly promises a reward of long life. Yet the boy falls from the tree and dies. "Where is his long life?" Elisha wonders, and abandons Jewish faith. His grandson Rabbi Jacob, a follower of Akiva, comments:

> There is not a single precept in the Torah whose reward is [stated] at its side which is not dependent on the resurrection of the dead. [Thus:] in connection with honoring parents it is written, "that thy days may be prolonged, and that it may go well with thee." In reference to the dismissal of the mother bird, it is written, "that it may be well with thee, and that thou mayest prolong thy days." Now, if one's father said to him, "Ascend to the nest, send away the mother bird, and bring me young birds, and he ascends to the nest, dismisses the mother bird, and takes the young, and on his return falls and is killed, where is this child's happiness and where is this child's prolonging of days? But in order that it may be well with thee, means on the day that is wholly good; and in order that thy days may be long, on the day that is wholly long. [that is, heaven].

And Rabbi Joseph adds: "Had Aher [Elisha] interpreted this verse as Rabbi Jacob, his daughter's son, he would not have sinned." But Elisha was incapable of understanding the verse like his grandson or like Akiva, because he's stuck in the *pshat*, the literal meaning of the verse, the surface interpretation of what we see and experience in the world. Only a theology which embraces human interpretive creativity can survive the world's harsh reality, and the Torah's seemingly empty promises. Akiva offers a world shimmering with infinite possibilities, just below the surface. Elisha's *pshat* world leaves us with death and tragedy.

===

Several years ago, my siblings and I were standing in a cemetery on a blustery winter morning in Kansas City, watching our mother's coffin being lowered into her grave. A brain tumor had killed her at age 61, at a time in her life when she'd overcome several hardships and was finally enjoying herself. Her untimely death screamed out "unfair" to her four children, as it does to countless families who've experienced similar tragedies. As the coffin plopped into the cold ground my sister leaned over to me and said "That's not her. That's not Mom." My brother, on my other side whispered, "Of course it's her. Where else would she be?" Later I thought, it's *pshat* vesus *drash*. My brother sees the surface reality. My mother's body died, we buried her, and there's no existence beyond the grave, nothing beyond the physical world, what we see and experience. My sister imagined another world, an alternate possibility, where my mother's essence was somehow separate from her body. Her corpse was no longer *her*, but *her* still existed, somewhere. "Imagined" is really the only word for it, since she couldn't touch this disembodied world, or measure it, or, of course, prove its existence.

Standing between my brother and sister, between *pshat* and *drash*, it occurred to me that I preferred the *drash*. I wanted to look at my mother's grave, now filling up with dirt shoveled in by the mourners, and see something other than the cold earth covering her coffin. At that moment, I *elected* to follow Rabbi Akiva. Not necessarily in his confident discovery of the afterlife in the mysterious words of the Torah, but in his way of reading the text and the world. This was my leap of faith: that there's more to reality than meets the eye, and that I could encounter an infinity of possibilities by studying Torah, which is to say, I could find God in the text, and therefore in the world. Post-modern faith demands these self-conscious leaps of belief. But it's easier for me to believe in God's presence in the text than that God parted the Red Sea, or that Jonah survived being swallowed by a big fish, or that God takes note of and cares about every moment of my life.

If Rabbi Akiva has an antagonist in the Talmud, it's Rabbi Eliezer, particularly in his understanding of the biblical phrase "eye for an eye." Several rabbis, following Rabbi Akiva's system, interpret the words creatively. "God forbid," they say of the *pshat*. The phrase actually means "the monetary value of an eye for an eye." But Rabbi Eliezer, seemingly directing his comment at Akiva, stubbornly insists *mamash*, or "Literally!"

And we can understand why. *Drash* wrenches words out of context and distorts reality. *Pshat* offers at least a surface intellectual integrity.

But *mamash* literally disenchants the world, robbing us of comfort, creativity and transcendence. It killed Ben Azzai and drove Ben Zoma to madness. It leaves Judaism, along with my mother, buried in the ground, unable to change or grow. I choose *drash*. The crowns in the letters beckon me every time my fingers move across the text. "Turn me and turn me," they whisper. "Everything is here."

Part Two

FICTION

Chapter Seven

Reb Moishe and the Beanstalks

Summer, 1995

IT WASN'T CATCHER IN THE RYE, or *The Foundation Trilogy*, or even Henry Miller that caught Moishe's attention. Unusual reading for a 13-year-old, but you didn't have to be a genius or even supremely precocious to enjoy JD Salinger, particularly at this expensive camp, filled with the offspring of doctors and lawyers. And certainly reading alone under a birch tree while most of her peers snuck off to dark corners to make out, or rushed to the lake for a quick swim, or just huddled together joking and giggling, boys with boys, girls with girls, waiting for the night, waiting for the changes that would transform them into adults—that wasn't so strange either. There were always teenagers—always adults for that matter—who preferred to be alone. But when he spotted her lugging around a thick volume called *Variety of Religious Experience*, and then saw her reading it under the tree, her lips moving slowly, he thought I should get to know this girl.

Until then, he'd spent his mornings sleeping late—he could sleep through anything, even Jewish tweens and teens howling like feral cats, playing and fighting with such equal fervor, Moishe could barely tell the difference. The rest of the day, into the evening, he stood on the front porch of his cabin strumming his guitar, writing new melodies, performing old songs. Most evenings, an audience of about 20 gathered—Tsippi and her clique of popular older campers, and a few curious counselors. It was Tsippi's mother, the president of the Camp's board of directors and a longtime fan, who'd gotten him the gig. They were paying him to hang out. Mingle with the campers, mentor the staff. But they'd given him nothing to do. No camp-wide performances, no classes, no lectures. Moishe understood. The camp director was a lifelong Conservative Jew, into Israeli politics, history, the satisfying logic of Jewish law, remembering the Holocaust. Moishe's mystical music, his reincarnation workshops, his lectures on Jewish paganism, on Torah and Tantra, his God-intoxicated calisthenics, his beard, his accent, his Yiddish pronunciations—they all struck this otherwise kind and competent fellow as not only nonsensical, but dangerous and subversive. And Moishe couldn't disagree—it was all those things, that was the point. Moishe flaunted the subversive nature of his teachings, and he couldn't deny that much of it was nonsense. This was religion after all, not physics.

Moishe suspected that Brother Director had also sensed the laziness that often infected Moishe's soul, and that's why he agreed to hire him. What harm could the old fat man do, sitting on the porch playing guitar all day? He couldn't exactly mesmerize these wealthy children with his thoughts on how *binah* mated with *chokhmah* to produce *tiferet*, or teach them to sit quietly and meditate on God's 39 true names, or explain how emanation, revelation, and creation were essentially the same things, the same powers clothed in husks of separate colors. It wasn't kid stuff.

It was only when he saw Yael—he'd learned her name from Tsippi—reading one day from William James, the next day from Kierkegaard, and the following day, God help her, from Heschel himself, that he thought, I wonder if I could talk to her? I wonder if I could teach her something? I wonder if I could do something here?

First he instructed Tsippi to bring her to that evening's front porch concert.

"Why?" Tsippi immediately asked.

He squinted at her through the thick lenses of his glasses. The 11AM sun, just emerging from a cloud, produced a kind of halo over Tsippi's head, while the glare obscured the rest of her body. An angel? Moishe wondered. But the cloud moved slightly, and Moishe took in the red tank top, the blue shorts, the bare feet, the eyes, so filled with scheming and petulance. A child, he thought, but then corrected himself. She's 16. Moishe's mother had gotten married at 18. And this Tsippi, his Tsippale? He had to admit she looked less like a child, more like her mother every day. He sighed. Careful, he thought. What was he doing here? Teenagers. They were a separate species. He knew nothing about them.

"Why Yael?" Tsippi asked again.

So beautiful. This stunning woman-child, perfectly formed, legs, torso, toes, wrists, fingers in perfect aesthetic alignment, proof of the Holy One's beneficence and artistry. And she stood under God's bright sun, His emanating touch, in this dazzling green Wisconsin paradise with rolling hills, blue lakes, butterflies and hummingbirds. God, God, God. So beautiful. Of course, there were the two reddish blotches on her nose, and the even bigger one taking up half of her lower chin. Her stringy, unwashed hair. There was the smell of chlorine, inescapable even in the kitchen. The latrines, the less said the better. The odor of boys, everywhere. The yammer and groaning of spoiled children. His aching back, re-injured every night by his ancient mattress. God. So wondrous.

"Nu, Tssipale, she's not a child of God? Like you, like me?"

"I don't have to do everything you tell me. Mom hired me to be your assistant. That doesn't mean you're my master. I'm not your slave."

"So, nu, you do it as a friend. I ask you as a personal favor. Your holy mother pays you money, that means nothing to me. For me, you're my Tsippale, my good friend."

She tilted her head. Her squinted eyes, her slightly upturned lips, they communicated annoyance and affection at the same time. How does she do that, Moishe wondered. So beautiful. If only she'd wash her hair.

"I wish you wouldn't call me that, Moishe," she said.

"Tsippale? I've always . . . "

"I'm not 7, Moishe. My name is Tsippora. And no one likes her. She's sort of creepy, reading by herself all the time. It's not a good idea. She'll keep people away."

He stroked his beard. Cliques, he thought. It's not that he was unaware. They existed even among the Yeshiva *bukhers*, in Yerushalayim. But those social rankings formed around Talmudic prowess, which meant Moishe was always at the top, in a category all his own. These rich American kids? The hierarchies were more rigid, and harder to follow than the sephirotic chart. He could ask Yael himself, but that would probably scare her away. "Nu," he said. "You're right, my Tsippale. Sorry, Miss Tsippora. I'm not your master. I'll discuss this with your mother. I'll need a new assistant. But please know, my love for you is the purest; it's undying, my sweet holy child . . . "

"Okay, okay. Chill. I'll do it. I wasn't *refusing*. Just giving you advice. She's not . . . well, look at her. She's not normal."

Moishe laughed, his belly laugh, his full-bodied chuckle. It worked for some people. For Tsippi's mother, and sometimes also for Tsippi. She laughed along with him, though Moishe wasn't sure why. "Normal?" he said. "Tsippale, does that seem like the criteria for what I'm doing here? You imagine I'm looking for normal?"

"Point taken," she said. She turned away quickly and sprinted, doe-like, across the field. Artemis, Moishe thought, the huntress in pursuit of prey. Or, better, our holy mother Rebecca, rushing forward because to live as God's prophetess is to rush, to move, to dart, to spring, to jump. So beautiful.

The breeze turned chilly that evening, so they moved indoors for the concert. Yael sat in the corner, her legs folded tightly against her chest, as if she was trying to pull herself into invisibility. But the room was small, and Moishe could see everyone, the older boys and girls, some of them holding hands or resting their fingers on a partner's thighs, all of them brushing up against each other, the physical contact contributing to the room's atmosphere as much as the music, maybe more so. And there was Yael, alone, tiny, but with budding breasts, just acquainting herself with adolescence. Moishe noticed the tears after the second song, and they flowed all through the concert, her hand in constant motion, brushing them away. Was it the music, he thought? Or the loneliness? What was the difference?

He assumed she would rush off afterwards; he'd have to find her the next day, under her tree. But she stayed, waited patiently, standing, leaning against the wall, while he hugged the older girls and boys goodbye, laying his hands on their dirty hair, whispering blessings into each of their ears. After the last one left, he approached her, held out his thick arms for a bear hug. But she stuck out her bony hand, and he understood right away. Nu, a handshake.

"The music was so beautiful," she said. "It reminded me so much of . . . "

She couldn't talk. No tears now, but no voice. She stared at his eyes, still holding his outstretched hand. His heart broke. He'd met adults moved to tears by his songs, hundreds of them. He'd embrace them in his famous bear hug, then sign them up for one of his courses, put them on the mailing list, maybe sell them a CD. But this wounded robin, this fragile soul? Could he do it? Could he be a rebbe to a lost teen?

"Child," he said. And it was enough. She wept, fell into his arms.

━━━

It wasn't so much the divorce, she told him. Divorce she could handle, half the kids in her class visited parents on the weekends. Even the adultery. She supposed she could live with that. Her father had at least tried to explain; her parents had fallen out of love with each other, it happened all the time. So, he'd reached out, in his pain and loneliness. To his secretary. Okay, creepy, but really who else was it going to be? She got it. She was mature. But the scandal. Her father's picture in the paper; the crazy headline accusing him of consorting with mobsters. It wasn't fair, she thought.

Her father wasn't a celebrity, just a rabbi. And now he was ruined. And humiliated. It would never go away. She knew it.

"Of course it will go away, sweet child. Everything passes." They were in Moishe's cabin, at the table he used for eating, though he had nothing to offer, no cocoa, no cookies. Just schnapps, but that wasn't for her. It was well past bedtime, but Moishe would explain to her counselor.

"Not this, Moishe. I can see it in my father's eyes. He's *so* embarrassed. His reputation means everything to him. It doesn't even matter if he gets another job. It's a stain. On his heart. I'm dying for him."

"You die for him. Gevalt. Child, that's not the way. He dies for you."

"I know. I know. And he would. But he's . . . he's not strong, Moishe. Not like you. He loves too deeply, that's what he told me."

He chuckled. "Ah, to love too deeply. I don't know. Nu, is this possible? But, sweet one, maybe it's you? Maybe you love too deeply? Or, you don't save enough love for yourself?" He looked at her, watched her study her fingernails, her eyes half shut. So focused. So tight. Was she thinking so hard about his cliches, his nonsense? Loving too deeply, what does that really mean? "Tell me something, my angel. Why Kierkegaard?"

She smiled. "You saw my books."

"Why do you think you're here? Nu, I get William James. Heschel, certainly. But Kierkegaard? Christian mysticism? Existentialism? I'm not seeing the connection between this and your beloved father."

"I'm trying to pray. It's all I can think of. It's not just for him. It's for my mother. She's so filled with hatred. I can't talk to her. About him, about anything really. And now we'll have to move. This is the thing, Moishe. I've got no control. I need to do something. I've prayed my whole life, but that was, well bullshit. Sorry. It was nothing. It's just bat mitzvah stuff. Memorizing. But the night before they made me come here, I saw my father in his office wrapped in a *tallis*, holding a *siddur*, swaying back and forth, and . . . I'd never seen him cry. But he was shaking. He was jerking around so much, the tears were literally flying off his face. It was the first time I ever thought that prayer could mean something other than getting the words right. He was praying like he could change things."

"And you want to? Nu? You want to change things."

"I want to pray. Like it means something."

"But you know, precious child. Everyone knows. What you want to change, can't be changed by prayer. You pray for what, nu, that your parents get back together? That you go back in time and stop them before they fall out of love? You've read Heschel too, nu? In prayer you enter the domain of the King. You feel the presence of the Sacred Queen. It's not a vending machine, you put in a shekel, it gives you a candy bar."

"I know, I know, I know, I know, I know." She grabbed a clump of tangled up hair and looked ready to tear it out. For the fourth or fifth time in the conversation, she seemed on the verge of hysteria. What, then, would Moishe do? But each time she swallowed back her tears. Instead of crying, her greenish brown eyes (he'd never seen that color in eyes, not sure he'd ever seen that color) beckoned, drew him in. "I swear, I'm not looking for that. I read your article on prayer in the *Jewish Handbook*. I just need . . . I want what you want. I know God won't put my family back together again. I'm *not* a child, not anymore. I want to believe someone's listening. I just want a presence. A voice. I swear, that's all."

Suddenly a buzzing sound filled the cabin, steadily increasing in volume. Yael brought her fist to her mouth, gaping at Moishe. Angels? Devils? "Mosquitos," he said. "Nu, they're exactly on time. Like alarm clocks, these dear friends. Except instead of calling me into God's beautiful world, they tell me it's time for bed. They only bite if I stay up too late talking to campers. That's the bargain I made." Moishe waited for her laugh, then shrugged. What did he know about how to make a 13-year-old girl laugh? But they'd connected, hadn't they? She'd read his article, his only non-academic publication, the only article he'd written that didn't attempt to unravel complicated Talmudic passages or compare different late medieval manuscripts. And he'd given her an idea. Maybe he could be useful in this place, with these children. Or at least with her.

He thought about how to approach Brother Camp Director about his proposed project, but then a brainstorm hit him of astonishing ingenuity: He wouldn't ask permission. He'd use some of his "free concert" time; sneak a few moments during lunch, and rely on the campers' discretion for the midnight sessions. He asked Tsippi to gather 10 campers, with only one criterion: They should be spiritual. Spirituality was key. *Mamesh* spiritual.

"I don't know anyone who's spiritual. No one is spiritual. I don't know what the word means. No one does. I don't know what *mamesh* means. Why do you always tell me things I don't understand? I don't want to work with you anymore. I don't like you."

She smiled through the rant, looking at the sky. Despite what she'd said, Moishe could tell she was considering who to ask, but perhaps using a different calculus than he'd suggested. Nu, it didn't matter. As long as one of the 10 was Yael. Tsippi wrinkled her nose at that, but didn't protest. In the end, she chose five boys and five girls. Except for Yael, they were all 16, athletic, confident, extroverted, awful, obnoxious, and, Moishe guessed, popular, though honestly, even when he became adored, massively adored years later, he never understood the concept.

This was the plan. The group planted two rows of beans at a corner of the central field. They'd care for each row equally—water, plant food, weeding, chasing away insects, fencing out squirrels and rabbits, whatever it took. He put the largest, most muscular boy in charge of cultivation because to Moishe he looked like a *shtarker*, a peasant. But they would only pray on behalf of one row. He instructed them to direct their hearts to "Row Avrum" in their morning and afternoon davening, and ignore "Row Itzik." And three nights a week they would gather for *khatzot*—midnight prayers, where they would pour out their souls for Row Avrum, and perhaps even throw in a curse at Row Itzik. He put Yael in charge of prayer.

She took to it like a demon. She composed hymns extolling God's loving mercy to beans planted in honor of our holy and saintly father Abraham. She convinced Moishe to set her words to melody and, in a surprisingly lovely voice, she led her congregation in heart-wrenching midnight sing-alongs. She distributed *tallis* and *tefillin* to everyone, and demonstrated how to tie *tefillin* to those who'd only done it once on their bar or bat mitzvah and forgotten. She carefully inspected the plants every morning, and when she spotted a few with suspicious-looking white spots, she adapted the traditional healing prayers and directed her campers to focus them on the sick individuals of Row Avrum. When that didn't seem to work—when one of the plants appeared to die—though Moishe himself wouldn't have been able to distinguish life from death when it came to beans—she switched to Debbie Friedman's modern healing song, changing the line "Bless those in need of healing" to "Bless those beans in Row Avrum in need of healing." When that didn't work, when it became clear even to farm-illiterates like Moishe that Row Itzik was thriving and Row Avrum was dying she instituted midnight *tachanun* services, where everyone threw themselves on the earth, their faces in the dirt. Together, as one sacred congregation, they implored the Holy One with all the breath in their lungs and all the blood in their veins, with full throats, as if their pleadings were the waters that fill the rivers and lakes, and their tears the holy salty substance that formed the seas. They implored the Blessed one of Mercy for healing, renewal, growth. But only for Row Avrum.

It didn't work. The campers emerged in the morning dusty and dirty from aerobic prayer, but Row Itzik sprouted deep green buds, and then the beginnings of actual beans, round, hard, healthy. Row Avrum—nothing. *Gornisht.* Some brown spots, leaves that vanished overnight, thin grassy stalks nibbled on by passing bugs, or withered in the Wisconsin sun. At first Moishe suspected sabotage. Was Tsippi sneaking to the field, poisoning the plants, adding spiders, or worms, or other plant predators? Did she dislike Yael so much, were the social hierarchies so ingrained that Tsippi would commit planticide to deny Yael any spiritual satisfaction, or alteration in her status? Yael, consciously or not, was becoming a leader in the project. The boys looked to her for prayerful guidance, and even the girls nodded respectfully at each liturgical instruction. Was this intolerable to his Tsippale? But Moishe noted a sad desperation even in Tsippi's normally cynical expression as the kids davened, and then faced the failure of their prayers. He didn't think Tsippi, or any of these American campers could effectively fake the existential sadness that he spotted behind their eyes. It wasn't sabotage. It was the verdict of God, The All Merciful. He'd rejected their prayers.

But that was the point, wasn't it? He wanted to demonstrate that davening was a spiritual experience divorced from outcomes. You came into the palace of the King—that was the only benefit to prayer. And that had to be enough. It was enough for him. He, after all, was not much more than a poor beggar, despite a lifetime of prayer. If God chose to heed our pleas, well, nu, blessed be God's name. But if the answer was no, still there was God. Prayer was God and God was prayer. So simple. So hard to explain. You explain by showing. That's what he did, to these sweet blessed children. He showed them.

It didn't go well. He broke their hearts. Tears, tears, tears. Protests, screams of agony. "I hate you!" Tsippi screamed, and Moishe nodded stoically. Of course. She hated him, not God. He hadn't rejected their prayers; he'd prayed along with them. But, nu, better they should hate Reb Moishe. They didn't get it. They wanted their vending machine to work. It didn't. They'd inserted their coins. But no candy for these sweet children. They cried that final midnight, beat their chests. They protested. "You tricked us! You killed the beans!" They called him a murderer, and he heard no irony at all in their accusations. What could he say? It didn't matter. It wasn't for them, after all. The next day, they'd be over it, back to flirting, to archery, to preening in ridiculously immodest bathing suits, to ball games he would never understand, to lives filled with trivial heartbreak and the American pursuit of happiness. Nu, even this drama, this gnashing of teeth, this sackcloth and ashes, what was it but a show, a school play like the dozens their parents were forced to watch as their privileged children grew into young Americans. Pretending.

But he spotted Yael, kneeling by herself, fingering a single stalk from Row Itzik. No tears, not yelling, just thoughtful contemplation. She gets it, Moishe thought. It's enough. I did it for her. But she didn't, apparently. Didn't get it. Two nights after the blow up in the field, just as the mosquitos announced his bedtime, she pounded on his door. It seemed she had stopped breathing. Her face was beet red and damp. Her lips trembled, but nothing emerged, no protest, no cry, no air.

"Gevalt," he said softly, and pulled her in by her arm. "Breathe, precious one," he said, and somehow it was enough. She expelled air, then sucked it in. Then collapsed in his arms, weeping. He patted her on the back of her tank top, careful to avoid the bare-naked arms. "Ah, sweet one. You care so much. The pain in your heart. That's what it means to enter God's throne room. That's our secret. You understand it now. But you already knew. My heroine. My strong one. You knew."

"No, no, no, no, no." She said, pulling back, staring at him, her brown-green eyes magnified by the tears, so they looked enormous, super charged. "I'm not strong. I failed. I saw what you were doing. I knew it wasn't about which row of beans did better. You told me. I read your article. Not about the outcome, that's what you teach. It's about entering God's palace. Being with God. I knew that. But, I just, I so, so, so, so, so, wanted those beans to live. I wouldn't even have cared if Row Itzik had lived, too. Or even if Row Itzik grew better beans. But my beans all died. It wasn't fair. I failed. It wasn't about the beans. It was me. I flunked. I can't pray." She fell back into his arms.

Weeping over spiritual failure. Who was this child? A reincarnation of the holy Rav Nahman? Nowadays, who mourned God's exile? Who grieved at the hiding of the face? No one. Except for this blessing in his arms, this *tsaddeket* with the broken home, broken heart. "You are my rebbe," he whispered to her. "Only a true rabbi teaches heartbreak, sweet one, and you're teaching me so much. So much light from the darkness. That's what you give me. It will come to you. The light will invigorate your soul. You'll be the truest friend, the wisest teacher, the most soulful lover. Gevalt, sweet friend. One day you'll see it."

But not that day. He couldn't console her. She was inconsolable. He walked her back to her cabin. Then detoured through the field to check on the plants. The fences were gone, torn away by rodents, or 16-year-old humans. The beans were eaten. Nothing left but a few stalks.

———

"What did you do to that girl?"

He was in the office of Brother Director. A cabin, not unlike his own, stained brown walls made of wood, a metal picnic table, kitchenette, ancient sofa. Moishe preferred bare walls, but the director decorated his with Israeli flags, posters featuring sand, camels, and blue skies; bearded Yeshiva boys in Jerusalem dancing, their faces turned toward heaven; soldiers weeping at the Western Wall; Israeli jet fighters flying over Auschwitz; campers in skimpy bathing suits cavorting in the lake, an advertisement for Camp Tikvah. Sitting at the uncomfortable table, the director peered down at Moishe, looming over him like a Cossack. The arms alone were tree trunks, but Moishe was particularly impressed with the huge barrel chest, the chest of a man who could hold his breath forever. Every limb on his body—his clenched fists, his coiled thighs, his bullet head, his sunburned face—communicated conflict. Imagine wrestling this man, Moishe thought. Could be fun for maybe three minutes.

"Do? Nu, I taught her some songs. She discussed with me this business with her family, her father. We davened, and, nu? She accuses me of something?"

The director leaned in. He threw his thick right upper arm across the metal table, as if challenging Moishe to an arm-wrestling match. Moishe noted the veins in his neck, now distended, nearly touching the arrow-sharp point of his chin. A hug, Moishe thought. This poor holy Jew needs a hug. Too much stress. Gevalt. "Moishe if she accused you of something, it wouldn't be just you and me talking. There'd be lawyers. And, listen, I can't believe you'd do anything truly inappropriate. So relax, okay, I'm not a cop. I'm not your biggest fan, I think you figured that out, but I'm not your enemy. The last thing we want is a scandal. But I have a camper who can't stop crying, can't get out of bed, and can only say two words. 'Reb Moishe.'"

Moishe shot to his feet. Not so easy for an out of shape *yid*, first thing in the morning. "I need to go to her."

"Sit. She's gone."

"Gone? Where is there to go?" He thought of the woods, the lake.

"Her father picked her up this morning. He's taking her for a ride. Hopefully, she'll come back."

"The father. But he . . . "

"Yes. Mendel Gold. He's got his own problems. But I've got a camper weeping her heart out, won't eat, won't get out of bed. What do you expect me to do?"

Expect? Interesting question. She calls for me, but instead this large fellow, my holy Brother Camp Director, calls her father? The problem *is* the father. The solution is spiritual, in her soul. There's no healing in running away. But how to explain the obvious, especially to this *gvir*, this wrestler. "Nu?" Moishe asked. "He came? They left? Gone? That's it?"

"Look, Rabbi Gold has been one of our biggest supporters. Frankly, he's raised a lot more money for us than Tsippi's mom. I know he's got problems now, but who knows where he'll end up. I wouldn't bet against him. His daughter has a break down, I call him. Right away. He wants to come, now, take her for a ride? Calm her down? I'm not going to argue. But I need to know. Because at some point she will stop crying. And then she'll talk. Moishe. Why is this girl crying? What did you do to her?"

Over the course of the next hour, Moishe told the story—in Moishe fashion, adding a few songs, even composing a new melody. Meandering through the details, whisking the listener on the magic carpet ride of story through the mystical cities of Bratzlav, Sura, Ishbitz, Mezrich, Stashov, Cleveland Heights. Because his audience of one was a literate Jew, he spoke in Hebrew and Yiddish and Aramaic, but always returning to English, this man's *mamaloshen*. Two rows of beans, one blessed, one cursed. *Nebekh*, the cursed one triumphed. Nu, like Esau. Like Ishmael. The hated brother, coming out on top. He referenced Rashi, Ramban, Radak, the Ritva zal. It was, Moishe thought, one of his better performances. Learned but, at the same time, moving. The head and the heart. Chochmah and Binah, in celestial harmony. The director listened intently, without interruption, never removing his beefy forearm from its position, a quarter inch from Moishe's.

Then he fired Moishe.

He gave him 24 hours to clear out his shit and hit the road.

———

Moishe assumed, as his 18-year-old Datsun struggled through the insanely green Wisconsin hills, that his career as a Jewish educator, such as it was, had ended. Even Tsippi's mother, he figured, would remove her patronage, since her own daughter would undoubtedly characterize herself as a victim of the bean plant scandal. He wondered if he should finally move to Israel, or maybe make a go of it in Poland, sell himself as the last real Eastern European Jew, travel the Jewish tourist circuit from Prague to Cracow to Budapest to Warsaw.

But, as was often the case when Moishe made predictions about his future, he was wrong. Far from destroying his livelihood, the beanstalks made him famous. The article he published on the experiment won several magazine awards. He turned it into a book, and then a documentary film. Concert bookings quadrupled, then quadrupled again. Tsippi's mother didn't abandon him after all, but instead recruited more millionaires, even billionaires. They clapped and danced and sweat and wept at his concerts; they took the business cards from his outstretched arms, and sometimes actually called him, for advice, or with new gigs, a concert, a lecture, a corporate class, spiritual consulting. In between concerts and lectures and workshops, in a kind of semi-sleep fugue state, he wrote serious scholarship on Jewish mysticism, and suddenly invitations came from serious universities. Case Western. Indiana. Northwestern. And, lastly of course, kicking and screaming, always resistant to mystical nonsense, the Hebrew Theological Institute. A faculty position. New donor friends insisted. Particularly the billionaires from the Valley of Silicon. They adored him.

And then, with God's good grace, Tsippi of all people became Chancellor. Her first academic act was to offer him tenure and an endowed chair. A big shot scholar at the age of 73, with some money in the bank.

That's what happened after Brother Director—Moishe honestly could never recall the holy Jew's actual name—fired him.

"What did you do to that girl?" the wrestler had asked, and Moishe told him the story.

But before the story he answered the question. "What did I do to her? I taught her how to pray."

Chapter Eight

Love, Murder, Plague: A Novella

I am not the one who loves
It's love that seizes me.

-LEONARD COHEN

April, 2020

FAMILY TIME! WE CAN play Monopoly. Scrabble. Ghost Fighting Treasure Hunters. Pictionary. Song Challenge with Alexa hosting. A backgammon tournament. Gin Rummy. Bullshit (but my mother called it "I Doubt It," which Sally and I prefer). Watch movies and shows on Netflix and Amazon Prime, but only the fun, friendly ones, because, really, isn't there enough stress right now, that we also have to worry about who shot Omar, or watch Offred get tortured for the millionth time? Or documentaries. That one about slavery and racism. Or the Ken Burns one, about baseball. Or the crazy guy who shelters all those cats (but on second thought maybe not that one). We can talk to each other. No, not about politics, or, if you must, limit the political talk to 20 minutes a day. Talk about the NBA. The Star Wars movies, particularly the seemingly disappointing final episode, that is perhaps deeper than we think. The new Star Trek show. A lot to analyze there! Take walks, but not just for exercise, not fast, fitness walks, but also not exactly strolls. Walks that pump the blood, but don't exhaust. Just walks. Even in the rain. Especially in the rain. Through the neighborhood, admire the surprising wide range of architectural styles, the Cape Cods, the Colonials, the Tudors, the Mid-century Moderns, the clapboards, the bricks, whites mostly, but also green and brown and red and even one purple. Cut through Mason's Ravine maybe even all the way downhill to Cataract Pond, stomp through the mud, look for goldfish, watch for snakes. Because walking is so good for you, physically, of course, but psychologically, even spiritually. What an amazing opportunity.

Just, you know, keep your distance. From people. Six feet, at least, though some say 12 or 15 or 30 feet. And wear a mask, maybe, if you can get one (but you can always make one!) because that's how you catch it. We think. Those innocent-looking folks, that fine family, on the same muddy path, they look healthy—here they are after all, basking in the great outdoors, hiking, just like you, some even jogging, their faces shiny with wellbeing. But you don't know where they've been, or where they go each day, where their hands have been, how they understand the term "social distancing." You can't see into their veins. Symptoms don't mean anything. We've heard. The asymptomatics. Those people may not be as cautious as us. So enjoy the blood pumping to your heart on this brisk, late winter day. Think positive thoughts. But veer sharply off the path, even into the marshy field, if you see people.

That proved impossible for Jacob, my youngest, three months passed his third birthday. He picked this season of quarantine to emerge from his lifelong wary introversion—where the sight of other people meant darting around quickly, looking for a place to hide, usually under my legs—into a chatty, curious, aggressively friendly social butterfly. "I wonder what their names are?" he'd exclaim, before jerking free from my hand and scampering ahead to greet the family of five coming toward us, each on silver scooters. They, naturally, recoiled from him as if he were a plague-carrying rat. They grabbed their scooters with one hand, and dispersed in a panic, each of the five, all in separate directions, even the kid who was shorter than Jacob. "I just wanted to know their names," he told me, when, breathless, I caught up with him. His lower lip trembled, the pre-tears tic he acquired his first month on earth. "No one wants to tell me their name."

It was after the fifth of the chasing Jacob episodes I realized that "Family Time" wasn't the most accurate euphemism for quarantine. No one liked Pictionary. Scrabble infuriated my older daughter Molly; she told us it triggered her SAT PTSD. Jacob shoved the backgammon checkers into his mouth and pretended to swallow (at least I think he was pretending). Star Wars exegesis left out my wife Sally who, in any case, as an essential worker, a radiologist, was too tired for games, and needed to remain at least six feet away from the rest of us. The twins, Justin and Jackson wrestled and screamed over which shows to watch, never once agreeing. And I couldn't bear another round of chasing Jacob through the neighborhood, tackling him before he could hug and kiss some stranger. One thing I learned from the plague: none of us was looking for more family time.

Anyway, there was an obvious solution. Shelter in place for us, and I assume for many if not most American families, meant the place where you sheltered was in front of some screen—a phone, a tablet, a laptop, sometimes the TV. By the second week, that's where we all stationed ourselves right after breakfast. Sally, six feet away, prevented even from blowing a kiss, waved at us then headed off to the hospital to save lives. And we all retreated to our mutual screens. Family time.

I was pretending to work—I was a fundraiser for a Jewish educational non-profit. But actually I was watching The Wire on my laptop, when my phone buzzed, notifying me of a Facebook message. "Why are you in Northampton?" It was from Ellie Klein, an unfamiliar name. And the photo was a white cat curled up next to a New York Giants mug, on an otherwise empty black desk. Spam, I thought, or phishing. Maybe an invitation to porn—something weird with the cat? The worst thing you can do is respond,

I reminded myself, as I stared at the cat's wide open yellow eyes. There was something about that cat. And it's not as if I was too busy on the job for a distraction. "Work?" I wrote back, and immediately the three dancing dots appeared. She was already composing a response.

"You don't work in Northampton."

I tried to think of a reply. I felt oddly attacked by this stranger, defensive about my choice of city, yet somehow moved to respond. I was about to explain the heated marital negotiations over Sally's job and my career, when the dots danced again.

"And why the question mark? Anyway, you work in Boston."

She knows me, I thought. I stared at the yellow-eyed cat, and felt its curious gaze, as if we were sizing each other up. "I work from home," I thumbed. "Only need to go to Boston once a week."

"I live in Northampton!"

So what? I thought. Thirty thousand people live in Northampton. And then, in virtually the same instance, I knew. Ellie was short for Eliana. Klein, I remembered, was the last name she now used; her mother's maiden name. It was Eliana. My hands trembled slightly, and I dropped the phone on the rug. When I picked it up, there was already a new message. "When can we get together?"

━━━━

Two hours later, after cleaning up the lunch dishes and playing a quick game of touch football with the twins in the backyard, I told Molly I was taking a walk, that she was in charge of her brothers. "Great!" Jacob yelled, bounding off of Molly's lap, running at me full speed, grabbing my leg. "Let's go! Can we see *people*?"

I looked beseechingly at Molly. She scowled, rolled her eyes, as if confronting heaven with the unfairness of it all. But, perhaps sensing an excuse to skip an online lecture, she decided to cooperate. She walked over slowly. "Come on, Jakey," she said, taking his hand. "We'll spy on people with my telescope. Daddy needs some time alone."

Alone? I thought, as I cut downhill through the neighbor's backyard, on my way to Childe's Park. It was chilly, about 50 degrees, but windy and dark, as if winter were coming on, not leaving. What is the feeling of six family members, in separate rooms in a sprawling, three-story house, being hypnotized by our screens every day for hours? I would call it loneliness, a peculiar, plague-induced, cyberage loneliness, but acute, nonetheless. I wasn't going to meet Eliana because I need to be alone.

The park wasn't empty. I spotted five dogwalkers, three with bandanas covering their faces, and one with a standard white medical mask. I searched through my coat pockets, but remembered that I'd left my keffiyeh drying on a closet peg. Two teenage boys tossed a frisbee back and forth. A group of four cyclists, in green and black bike gear and bare faces pedaled around the pond, barely two feet from each other. From the same family, I thought. Or just stupid and careless. Birds hopped and flittered, squirrels darted. A young African American woman pushed an elderly white man with an impressive mane of gray hair in a wheelchair. Both wore scarves wrapped tightly around their faces as if this were mid-winter Alaska, and not early Spring in New England. So there was life in the park, yet it was still ghostly quiet. The dogwalkers didn't coo or sing to their dogs, the frisbee tossers focused mutely on catching and throwing, the wheelchair pusher stared straight ahead, like a watchman on a tower. It was as if the social distancing rules included a sound component—a safe distance, but also no talking, humming, grunting, no breaking the isolation spell with needless noise, no sounds. Even the birds seem to cooperate. Even the wind.

Eliana wasn't wearing a mask. I would have recognized her anyway, but a mask might have buffered the electric force of recognition. She looked exactly the same. Straight black hair, shoulder length. A blush of red on her cheeks, as if she were perpetually embarrassed by something. Remarkably, no wrinkles I could see, though she was almost exactly my age—42. Identical black peacoat or, if not the same one from 18 years ago, or 13 years ago, an exact duplicate. She was watching her phone intently when I spotted her, sitting ramrod straight at the picnic table. She didn't look up until I stopped at what seemed to me was exactly six feet away. Six feet of distance, I thought. A good practice for meeting up with an old girlfriend. She looked up and smiled sadly. White teeth, I thought. Perfect white teeth.

"Peter," she said. Her voice was soft, as always, but in the still silence of the park, of the world, it sounded too loud. She didn't get up. We'd both fallen into the habit of non-physical greetings, no touching elbows, no fist bump, certainly not a hug or kiss, even when facing an old lover. Good rule, I thought, again.

"Eliana," I said, and almost stumbled on the third syllable of her name. I wasn't used to saying it. Obviously, the name was forbidden at our house. I circled around her, keeping a safe circumference, and sat at the opposite corner of the picnic table.

"You look exactly the same," I said.

She nodded. "That's what people tell me. I get carded sometimes, at grocery stores. Grad students ask me out, they figure I'm in my 20s." She shrugged. "Won't last forever. I can tell you I don't *feel* 23." She studied my face for a bit too long a time. As if she were about to paint my portrait and had to make a difficult decision about what to do with my nose. "You look good," she decided.

I chuckled. "Not 23," I said. "Or 28. It's been almost 15 years. I'm middle-aged."

"Why are you here?"

So much for small talk. But that was Eliana. Rabbinical school friends who knew both of us well warned me she seemed to be on the spectrum, oblivious to social cues, impatient with any activity that wasted time, especially humor and useless chatter. I ignored them because I'd fallen in love with her. And anyway, for over a year she did open up to me, after a fashion, expressing a surprising and dramatic range of emotions. Of course, she also kept her secrets.

"Why am I here?" I answered. "It was your idea. I'm here because you wanted to meet."

"You know what I mean."

There it was, the tone. An accusation. I wasn't just imagining it from her Facebook texts. Predictably, I felt guilty, a not uncommon feeling for me, and not at all surprising right then, considering who I was meeting with. But what an odd accusation.

"Sally got a job offer here." I shrugged. "Her job brings in a lot more money than mine. So we live here, and I commute. But just once a week."

"That's it? It's because of Sally? That's your story?" She looked at her phone and frowned. I remembered that she had a particularly difficult time meeting my eye when I annoyed her. But none of this made sense. I could think of all sorts of reasons why she might still be angry with me. But why did I owe her an explanation for where I lived?

"It's not a story," I said. "It's just how things worked out."

"How things worked out. That's what you're calling it. You and I both in Northampton. With her right up the road."

"Her?"

"You really don't know what I'm talking about? It's all just a weird coincidence?"

"Wait," I said. "Why are *you* here?"

She shook her head, and shut her eyes. "You don't know? You really don't know?"

"Eliana. I don't know what you're talking about." I'd imagined or feared or fantasized a reunion with Eliana for some time, but the fantasies never went this way, with her pissed off, and talking in riddles.

She opened her eyes, wide enough that I could see the wrinkles just below her dark eyebrows. "I'm here because of my mother," she said.

I felt a chill. Stupid, I thought. So stupid to respond to her texts, to agree to meet her. "Your mother lives in Northampton?" I said. "How is that possible?"

She laughed bitterly. "Well, not exactly Northampton. Not the Northampton you live in."

And I got it. "The jail," I said. The county jail was just across the border, in Easthampton.

"The state prison in Deering got too crowded. With the Pandemic. They moved the non-violent prisoners to county jails. The one here is the least crowded."

"Non-violent?" I said. Eliana's mother had been convicted of killing her husband, Eliana's father, with an axe.

Eliana smiled. "It's a relative term."

August, 2007

I met Eliana's mother Judith the day before the funeral service for her husband. My college roommate Andy inherited a Jewish mortuary on the Upper East Side of Manhattan, and he would often throw funerals my ways, unaffiliated folks, without family rabbis. "I think you'll enjoy this one," he told me over the phone. It was a humid August morning in Manhattan. I'd only been walking for 10 minutes, from my apartment to Madison Avenue Synagogue where I was assistant rabbi, and I was already sweating through my suit. "And not just the money," Andy said, "though I imagine you'll get plenty of that."

"Enjoy?" I said. "Andy, it's a funeral. I appreciate the referral, but, really . . . "

"It's Carlos Epstein. The deceased."

He waited for a response. The name rang a bell. "Who? Sounds familiar, but I don't . . . "

"Look him up," he said. "Better yet, read today's paper. Not the Times. The Post, or the Daily News. Then come on over. I'll introduce you to the lovely widow."

I bought a Post from the newsstand at 84th and Madison, right outside the synagogue. "Millionaire Mob Boss Murdered" was the screaming headline. Underneath the bold type: "Felled by Axe Behind Luxury Building." The article described Epstein as "the last of the storied Jewish mobsters, part of a gang that came to America from Cuba, bringing with them an expertise in prostitution, drugs, gambling, extortion, and murder. Epstein bullied his way to the top of the gang through a conniving street brilliance, occasional charm, and mostly an unmatched murderous ruthlessness. He served three years at Rikers Island for cutting off a drug customer's nose."

I called Andy from the lobby of the shul. My heart was beating too rapidly to climb the stairs to my office. "A mob boss? A killer? That's who you hooked me up with? I'm supposed to say nice things about him? Bemoan his loss?"

"He's not a child of God? He doesn't deserve a funeral?"

"Andy, it says in the Post he ordered the killing of maybe a dozen people. Before that he murdered seven people with his own hands. Two of them with a knife."

"Look, Peter. You owe me. How much business have I thrown your way?"

"Andy, I'm a rabbi. It's not business."

"You don't like the money? Five hundred bucks a pop. You don't need it? You give it away? Now look, I need a favor from you. Honestly, no other rabbi will want to touch this funeral. But you'll appreciate it. Trust me."

I looked around the lobby. It was early, just past seven—only me and the security guard were there, though soon the morning service regulars would file in. I still had to look over that day's Torah reading. "Okay, Andy, okay. A favor. For you."

"Appreciate it. You read the article? The whole thing?"

"The first two paragraphs were enough."

"Read the whole thing. To the end. Then get over here after minyan. I need you to meet with the wife."

Still damp with sweat, I ducked into the downstairs men's room, and flipped ahead in the paper to read the rest of the article. It didn't take long to find the part Andy wanted me to read. Apparently, "according to experts on the Jewish-Cuban mob," these Manhattan gangsters didn't execute rivals by swinging axes at skulls. Too violent, too attention grabbing. The method of choice was a simple bullet to the head, usually in a car so they could dump the body in a convenient place. Unnamed sources at NYPD confided to the Post reporter that this particular murder had the markings of a rage killing, a crime of passion, not business. So despite Epstein's violent past, said the source, it's likely he was done in by an intimate acquaintance—a disgruntled family member, or a lover. In fact, the number one suspect in the case was Epstein's wife, Judith.

=====

I found Andy and Judith, the wife/chief suspect, in the funeral home's largest family room, a dark-wood-paneled, half-a-ball-room-sized gathering place filled with stuffed couches, thick oak end tables with drawers, and heavy lounge chairs. A strange place for a meeting of two people, but maybe Andy was trying to impress her. He was pouring an amber liquid into Judith's water glass when he saw me walk in. He quickly shoved the whisky bottle into a drawer and stood up. Judith knocked back the drink in one motion.

"Ah, Peter," Andy said. "I mean Rabbi Greenberg." Andy was a short, stubby guy, less than 5 foot 6, and probably 200 pounds—"Stubby" was actually his nickname at Northwestern, though I was careful not to use it around his paying customers—but he was surprisingly athletic and graceful. He danced over to me and grabbed my elbow with a meaty hand, pulling me quickly toward Judith, as if I were a fish trying to shake off the hook. Judith stayed quiet on the sofa and looked down when Andy introduced us. She ignored my outstretched hand, as if she didn't see it, as if it wasn't there.

"Okay, then." Andy said, shrugging. I dropped my arm. "I'll leave you two to it."

I thought about sitting beside her on the sofa, but decided instead to haul over one of the heavy chairs and plop it down next to the couch.

"Mrs. Epstein," I said. "I'm sorry for your loss."

Her face shot up. She studied me. She was an attractive woman, long black hair, wrinkle-free complexion, thin, but not skinny. I spotted something vaguely familiar in her dark brown eyes. "You're sorry?" she said. "Sorry? Why would *you* be sorry, Peter?"

I could see she'd been crying. Both eyelids were swollen and red, and her cheeks were still damp. "Um, well, I mean, I'm sorry you're experiencing grief. Or pain."

"But you don't know me, do you, Peter?"

"I don't," I answered. "But, um, well, it seemed like a polite thing to say. It's, uh, kind of an expression."

As I stumbled through that sentence, I noticed three tiny, ball-bearing-shaped tears flow from the corner of her left eye down her cheek. She didn't look like an axe-wielding murderer. First of all, she was short, maybe 5'4". She would have had to leap, or at least stand on her toes to smash in a normal size man's head. And that's assuming she'd have the strength. Her arms were unusually twig-like, scraggly, breakable. Then there was her obvious grief, the red eyes, the ball-bearing tears. Would a murderer weep over her victim? Maybe. I'd never met a murderer before.

I took a deep breath. Do the work, I told myself. It's not your job to solve the murder, or punish the killer. The woman in front you lost her husband and is looking to you for guidance on the funeral. Focus. "Tell me about your husband," I said.

She stared at me wide-eyed, tiny tears still flowing down her left cheek.

Stupid, I thought to myself. Even if she didn't kill him, she must have known he was a vicious criminal. What could she possibly say about a man who served time for slicing off someone's nose?

"He was a saint," Judith said.

"Excuse me?"

"A saint. Did you not hear me, Peter? Oh, I know we don't have saints in our religion. I just—what would be the word? He was righteous. Is there a Jewish word?"

"Um, well, why don't you tell me what you mean? How was he righteous?"

"You know the homeless? The homeless people? The ones on the street? You know them?"

"Well, I, sort of. I know who you're talking about."

LOVE, MURDER, PLAGUE: A NOVELLA

"He loved them. So generous. Every time we passed one on the street, on the way to dinner or the theatre, he'd give them money. Not coins, money, bills. He would take out his roll and peel off 20s, sometimes 50s. I don't think he even looked at the denominations. He just loved them. He was righteous."

"Wonderful," I said. I waited, watched her face. She was looking toward the door, as if expecting someone to arrive. Then she turned back to me and blinked, as if surprised I was still there. Ball-bearing tears now rolled down both of her cheeks. I handed her the box of tissues, but she ignored it, and made no attempt to wipe her face.

"That's all," she said. "I think you have enough for a eulogy, don't you, Peter? Anyway, if you need more material, you can always read the newspapers."

Was she screwing with me? Calling him righteous when the newspapers made clear he was a violent criminal? I decided it didn't matter. Not my job.

I explained the funeral service to her, the timing, the liturgy, the choreography. She looked at the door the whole time, occasionally nodding, though it wasn't clear what she was nodding about. I told her about *kriah*, the ritual tearing of a garment performed by the immediate family. "Any other family?" I asked. "Children, siblings? Parents?"

"Oh, no," she said quickly. "No one else. Just me."

"You didn't have children?" I asked.

"Of course, we did," she said. "We were married. We have a daughter."

"But she won't be at the service?"

"Of course she'll be at the service. She's my daughter."

I nodded. Drugs, I thought. She's medicated. Grief is stressful. And so, I thought, is murder. "You and your daughter. No one else?"

"No, no, no one else. Well. Of course. There's Ida." She shrugged, then giggled. "She hates me," she said. A single tear rolled down her right cheek.

"Ida," I said.

103

"Carlos' sister." She smiled for the first time then looked at the ceiling, as if lost in thought, nostalgic. "She hates me," she said. She turned her face slowly back to me. "Can I ask you a question?"

"Of course."

"Carlos is speaking to me. Right now. Can they do that? I mean, the dead? Talk to us? Is that allowed?"

"Allowed?"

"You know, Peter. Kosher. Is it kosher for Carlos to talk to me, now, when he's dead?"

"What does he say?" I asked, and them immediately regretted the question.

"Well, I don't think that matters, does it? That's not important. And really, Peter, it's none of your business."

"No, of course not."

"Can you tell him to stop? Stop bothering me. He'd listen to you. He liked rabbis. I think he wanted to be a rabbi, if I'm remembering correctly."

"Mrs. Epstein, I don't think . . . "

"Calm down, Peter. I'm just joking. I don't expect you to speak with him. It's just that—I wish he'd stop talking to me. Maybe after the funeral. Can we just—can we do it right now?"

"The funeral? It's on the schedule for tomorrow. I'm not sure Andy can change it. I think the police still have the body . . . "

"The police?"

I pictured a coroner's office, burley policemen, ambitious prosecutors surrounding the cadaver, examining the axe wound. "Well, I think . . . "

"Oh, it doesn't matter. We'll do it tomorrow. No one else will show up, anyway. Why would they? It will probably just be the two of us. Me and Carlos." She smiled at me, her cheeks still wet with tears. "Just me and my husband. And you, of course, Peter."

———

In fact, close to a thousand people pushed their way into the funeral. When I arrived, a half hour before the service, there was already a logjam of mourners crowding the entrance. Andy signaled to me to come around back to the rear entrance. I pushed through a pack of reporters, and flashbulbs exploded in my face. Andy grabbed my elbow and tugged me into the building, slamming the door behind him. He held on tightly as he guided me into a family room, and introduced me to Ida Epstein, sister of the deceased. Then his phone buzzed, and he slipped out. I watched the tall, gray-haired, middle-aged woman, with a black dress and black shoes, stare out the window, watching the crowd.

"Rabbi Green," she said, still facing the window.

"Uh, actually it's Greenberg. Rabbi Greenberg. I mean it doesn't matter, but my last name is Greenberg. Not Green."

She faced me. "The newspaper said Green. Robert Green. That's not you?" There was a Daily News on the coffee table. She picked it up and showed me the front page. "Mob Boss Funeral" was the lead headline. Ida pointed with her thumb to a line at the bottom of the page. "Family rabbi Robert Green will lead the service." She flipped ahead. I was astonished and mortified to see a picture of myself leaving the funeral home. It looked like I was rushing, like I couldn't get out of there fast enough. "That's not you?" Ida asked.

"No, no, it is me. It's just that it's not my name. My name is Peter Greenberg." I decided not to clarify that I also wasn't, in fact, the "family rabbi."

"Then why does it say Robert Green?"

I shrugged. "Green, Greenberg, easy mistake, I guess. And Robert? I don't know. I don't even know any Roberts."

She studied me. She was taller than I, so she had to tilt her head down, which somehow added to the impression of haughty curiosity. Who was this idiot, she seemed to be thinking, and why did he feel it necessary to lie about his name? Anxious to change the subject, I was about to express my condolences when she said, "She killed him, you know."

"Excuse me?"

"Judith. She murdered my brother. It's obvious. She's wanted him dead for a long time. I personally heard her threaten him on three occasions." She shook her head, clenched her right fist, and glared at the wall. "I should have seen this coming, gotten him away from her. I just didn't think . . . an axe? My God." She turned back, faced me, and waited for a response. But what was I supposed to say? I wasn't the police. My only task was to get through the day and tell Andy to take me off his list when it came to Jewish gangsters. "She *killed* him," Ida repeated, and for the first time I noticed a slight accent, as if an accusation of murder brought out the Cuban in her. "She *keeled* him," she said once again. But then added a sentence I didn't see coming. "And he was a saint!"

We stared at each other, but then turned quickly as we heard a doorknob rotating, a door squeaking. Someone was entering the room. Judith, I thought. What happens now? Will Ida slug her with her still clenched fist? Will Judith defend herself with an axe? But it wasn't Judith, though for a split second I wondered how she'd gotten so young overnight. It was Eliana.

2002

I met Eliana in Jerusalem, my first year of rabbinical school. She was a grad student at Hebrew University, studying Yiddish literature. A mutual friend invited both of us to a Seder. Much to my delight, she was seated next to me, though she barely said a word through the ritual, the learned discussions, the meal. Shy, I thought. Or, just as possible, she doesn't like me, doesn't appreciate my extroverted inclination to fill every silence with talk. I told her about my newfound interest in Jewish mysticism, my job at the Empire Hotel cleaning bathrooms, my favorite guitarists. I even tried out the little Yiddish I'd learned from my grandfather. That was the only thing that got a response—a slight smile and a correction.

She surprised me by asking me to walk her home. It was 2AM, the Seder had stretched to over six hours. Other than to give directions, she didn't talk at all on the half hour walk. But she did laugh at my jokes, and seemed to listen as I pointed to street signs and explained how Jerusalem's avenues and alleyways got their names. And she astonished me by kissing me on the cheek when we reached her apartment. I was too surprised to ask for her phone number.

So I stalked her. I wouldn't have used the word back then, but how else to describe walking past her apartment three, sometimes four times a week, sometimes twice in one day, hoping to run into her? Finally, about a month later, on a sunny May day, she spotted me from her balcony and waved me over.

That day, we walked the length of the city, from her apartment in Rehavia, through the Center of Town, down the hill to Jaffa Gate, through the crowded Arab market to the Jewish Quarter and the Wall, back through the fragrant Armenian Quarter, out Zion Gate, down the winding, stone steps through the Hinnom Valley, up the ramp past the ultra-modern Cinemateque, through the stone houses in the Mishkenot Sha'ananim artist quarter, up-hill through the traffic clogged Derekh Bet Lechem, past the basketball courts in Liberty Bell Park, to the bustling narrow lanes of The German Colony, then a right on Hamelitz, up the stairs to my apartment into my bedroom. She talked most of the way. About Yiddish Literature. The underappreciated Chaim Grade, a thinker with the range of Tolstoy; Eliana pointed out his second home on Lincoln Street, where his ancient embittered widow still lived. She characterized Isaac Bashevis Singer as overrated, obsessed with demons and sex, in that order, and the less said, the better. She held forth on poets I never heard of. I regretted that I'd pretended to speak Yiddish at the Seder, because she peppered her conversation with Yiddish phrases that I pretended to understand, mostly by laughing, since Yiddish struck me as funny, even though I didn't understand a word.

After Yiddish, she turned to politics. She surprised me with right-wing views. She despised then-president George Bush, but only because he'd gone soft, pushing amnesty for illegal immigrants, expanding government in ruinous ways, and refusing to attack Iran. Her political hero by far was Bibi Netanyahu; she trusted him never to give an inch. Arik Sharon, she said, who contemplated a partial withdrawal from Gaza and the West Bank, should probably be killed. I chuckled when she said that, and she smiled. Kidding, I thought. There was a surprising sensual ardor both to her political views and her passion for Yiddish culture. Her voice turned deep and resonant, like a leading lady in a noir film, and her face blushed slightly. I didn't agree with her politics and never cared much for Yiddish, and she never sold me on either subject. But I loved listening to her, loved watching her body as she gesticulated dramatically, like an orchestra conductor.

She said nothing about herself, her family, her background, even though I asked her three or four times. Oddly, it didn't seem like she was ignoring my questions. She would begin to answer, and then pivot seamlessly to a point about Sholem Asch and his Christian heresies, or Sholem Aleichem's deceptions, or how much she admired Donald Trump and Bill O'Reilly. Fox News talking points mixed with literary theory. Somehow, I fell for it.

For the next year, back in New York, continuing our studies, Eliana regaled our friends with our "meet cute," how a month after the Seder she just happened to be on the balcony at the exact moment I chose to go for a walk in her neighborhood—an especially blessed coincidence, she'd point out, since she'd discovered I didn't really like going for walks. I never corrected her, even after I asked her to marry me, and she accepted with tears and a joyful hug, because, in retrospect there was something creepy about my endless walks past her balcony.

The day after she said yes to my marriage proposal, she broke up with me, over the phone. I should have seen it coming; almost everyone close to me—my parents, my brothers, my closest friends—warned me. Too much secrecy, or unexplained weirdness. I never met her family. She told me she was an only child and that she'd cut off her parents, but she wouldn't tell me why. In fact, it took six months of asking to elicit one simple sentence about her parents: "They're out of the picture." Two months later, she added two words: "Not dead." She didn't get mad at my curiosity, didn't sigh, or fume, or storm off. She'd just smile her half smile, and change the subject, pretend that we were really discussing the Iraq War or 9/11 or the pathetic Democrats. I always backed off because I was afraid of provoking anger, even though she never once snapped at me, or showed any sign of impatience. The closest she came to anger—a raised voice, squinty eyes, finger jabbing her desk—was when discussing Sholem Asch, and his Yiddish Christian novels. We never quarreled. That in itself was weird.

Also, she disappeared, frequently, for days at a time. Just had to get away, she'd tell me. I'd offer reasons: "An academic conference? Family reunion? Health treatments? Writer's retreat?" She'd smile or even laugh and show me an article she'd seen in Commentary Magazine, or ask me about my advanced Talmud class, or just hum and make dinner. She'd speak less the day after returning from these mystery trips, send all phone calls to voice mail, stare out the window with a half-smile, yawn frequently, go to sleep earlier, wake up later. The visits away were either exhausting or traumatizing or refreshing. It was impossible to say. She never revealed a single detail.

Which was how she broke up with me. No details, no reasons. Just five words, as soon as I answered the phone: "We need to break up." I pretended not to hear her correctly. "My voice is breaking up?" I asked, forcing her to repeat herself. I asked why, and she went back to the five words. I tried to guess at reasons. Her parents objected. She couldn't marry a rabbi because she wasn't religious. She was afraid of starting a family since hers had imploded. She breathed softly into the phone after each guess, never hanging up, but never saying anything beyond the five words. I grew more upset, then hysterical as the phone call dragged on. I promised to change, though I had no idea what needed changing. "Just talk to me!" I screamed. "Talk! Talk!" Her breath quickened. I imagined she was crying, though, in fact, I'd never seen her weep. After 45 minutes of whiny speeches from me, and even-keeled five-word responses from her, I hung up. I had the feeling she would have listened quietly for hours, waiting me out, never hanging up, but never giving anything except the one sentence she repeated mechanically, like a phone's digital voice.

I grieved for months. Lost weight. Skipped classes. Went on long, evening walks through Central Park, breaking down in tears when I spotted lovers holding hands. I told myself I could accept it if only I knew why. I phoned Eliana several times a day, but she never picked up, and after three months, she changed her number. I stalked her midtown apartment waiting outside the building, sneaking past the doorman, and knocking on her door. But a neighbor told me she'd moved and didn't know where.

It wasn't real, I told myself. It's obvious now. She never opened her heart to you; you never won her confidences. This wasn't intimacy, not for her. It was companionship, at best. After three months, I talked myself into the utter insubstantiality of the relationship. It wasn't real, so it shouldn't hurt so much. Maybe the pain will prove just as ephemeral as the affair.

It helped that I'd met Sally, a fourth-year Columbia med student. On our first date, she told me all about her family, her brother and sister, her doctor parents. She had zero interest in right-wing politics, never watched Fox News, and knew less Yiddish than I. Six months after our first date, I asked her to marry me at a small Israeli restaurant on 74th Street. She smiled widely and whispered "Yes." We got married in Cleveland, her hometown, three months later. Ten months after that we welcomed Molly, our first child. Sally interned at Columbia Presbyterian; I got a job as assistant rabbi at the biggest Conservative synagogue in New York. We lived on 94th and 3rd, surrounded by young, successful Manhattanites. I never saw Eliana, never heard from her. I thought of her often. I Googled her at least once a week.

August, 2007

Eliana stared at me from the entrance to the family room, and shook her head quickly. A sign? But what was it supposed to mean? It didn't matter because I was paralyzed, dumbstruck. It couldn't be her, not now during this bizarre funeral, but there she was. I was hit by a sudden memory of Judith's eyes, and I put the pieces together. Judith was Eliana's mother. So her father was—the mob boss, the murderer. Several facts jammed into place in my mind, while my body, and luckily my tongue, remained frozen.

Ida strode across the room and embraced Eliana. "I'm so glad you're here."

"Where's my mother?" she asked Ida, ignoring me.

"You think I know? You know what happened, dear. You know she killed him."

"Aunt Ida. Please."

"You know! Even the rabbi knows. Ask him. He knows." Ida turned to me, while Eliana finally opened her brown eyes widely and stared. "She killed him." Ida said, in a whisper that carried across the room. "And he was a saint."

Just then, Andy poked his head into the room and told us it was time to start. Judith was waiting in the chapel, in the front row. We marched in together. Eliana took the seat next to her mother, Ida sat directly behind Judith. I walked slowly to the podium, then shuffled my notecards, opened the prayer book, took a breath, and looked up. Just to my right, I saw a group of scruffy, jeans-clad men and women leaning in, and pointing recording devices at me. Reporters, I thought, more than a dozen. Lining the wall to my left stood ten men in identical black suits with black ties, wearing sunglasses, even though we were indoors. FBI? I thought. Security? The rest of the huge crowd looked like typical Manhattan mourners, well-tailored, bejeweled, fit, chatting to each other, waiting for me to begin. I was about to when my eye caught a young attractive blond hurrying into the room and sitting next to Aunt Ida. The mistress, I thought. The Daily News that day had quoted a source explaining Judith's alleged motive for slaughtering her husband: an affair with a "hot young blond." Ida handed her a handkerchief and she dabbed her eyes. I was surprised to see a number of mourners, all through room, touching their eyes and nose with Kleenex. People were crying over this killer.

In my eulogy I emphasized that "we are not here today to stand in judgment." The Daily News (page 1) called my remarks "powerful and heartfelt." I mentioned Epstein's philanthropy, pointed to his empathy with the homeless, shared Ida and Judith's assessment that he was a saint. The Post (page 14) attacked my words as "stumbling, inauthentic, and frankly preposterous."

After I concluded the service with the Mourner's Kaddish, Andy rushed up to me and the family and hustled us out a side door. "Reporters all over the place," he told us. "Paparazzi. And cops. Here's what we'll do." He'd hired a blond actress to pretend she was the young and beautiful mistress. Andy sent her out on to Madison Avenue, into the pack of reporters. They pounced, screaming questions at her and snapping photos, while she hurried into one of Andy's black limousines. "That's the decoy," Andy explained. "They're headed for the Bronx. We'll get you all out the back way."

Eliana rested her head against the window the moment we entered the limo and slept the whole way to the cemetery. Judith peppered me with questions about the life of a rabbi. "Something I once considered," she told me, watching her daughter sleep. "It's not too late, do you think?" Ida glared at her, and she shut up. It was quiet the rest of the way.

Andy's "switch the limo" trick didn't seem to work. At least 20 reporters and photographers waited for us at the gravesite, snapping photos, barking out questions: "Why'd you kill him?" "Was it because of the blond?" "What are you worth now?" "Where's the axe?" Andy punched a few buttons on his cell phone and within minutes two NYPD cars pulled up, and the cops cleared away the reporters. After the last one left, an unearthly silence descended. Andy waited in his car, while the rest of us slowly climbed a steep green hill. We were just four now—me, Ida, Judith, and Eliana—facing a yawning wound in the earth, and a mound of brown soil. I hurried through the burial liturgy, then we each grabbed a shovel and threw in the customary token of dirt. As we walked back to the cars—I'd be driving back with Andy in his Toyota—Ida leaned down and, with hot breath, whispered in my ear, in a volume that everyone heard, "She killed him." Judith glared at her sister-in-law with an expression so filled with hate, it could only be used on the most intimate of acquaintances.

Two days later Judith showed up unannounced at my office. Her long black hair was unwashed and stringy, and she wore the same black dress she wore at the funeral. I wondered if she'd showered or changed in two days, or, for that matter, slept. There were dark puffy bags under her eyes, as if someone had slugged her.

None of which is to say she looked unattractive. I found her weirdly alluring, like a lost princess, Beauty escaped from the Beast. Or maybe I was just struck by her resemblance to Eliana. I was busy—sermons to write, pastoral calls to make, programs to plan, classes to teach, not to mention a 3-year-old daughter at home and a mostly absent wife, toiling through her radiology residency at Columbia Presbyterian. I had no time for Judith Epstein, #1 suspect in the murder of her husband and, anyway, not a member of the congregation. But I ushered her in, sent my assistant for coffee, and moved around my desk to sit next to her.

"You never answered my question," she said. She tilted her head down, toward the carpet.

"Uh, sorry. I don't . . . "

"About the dead. Can the dead speak to the living?"

I looked at her eyes, the dark bags, the constant blinking. Drugs, I thought. She's obviously on something. Naïve of me not to think of that immediately. She's delusional. "No," I said firmly. "The dead don't speak to the living. I mean, we have memories, and we can imagine what they might say . . . "

"No, no. I don't mean that. That's obvious, Peter. Psychobabble. I'm talking about real communication. From, you know, the other side of the curtain."

"Doesn't happen," I said.

"You're so sure?"

I shook my head. "Mrs. Epstein. I think maybe you need . . . "

"Oh, never mind," she said. "That's not even why I came. I just wanted to give you this." She took an envelope out of her purse and handed it to me. Then she stood.

"Mrs. Epstein," I said. "It's not necessary." Andy paid me $500 for the non-member funerals, a cost he passed along to the customer. I got up and tried to hand her back the envelope.

She smiled. A ball-bearing tear leaked from her left eye and traveled slowly down her cheek. "It's not about the money, Peter. Please, just take the envelope."

I nodded, shook her hand. Then she left. I went back around my desk, sat at my chair and stared at the envelope for five minutes. Then I opened it. There was a check for $18,000. Not about the money, I thought. I considered my options. I was under no obligation from the synagogue to return the money. But the deal with Andy was that he paid me, not the mourners. I was about to call him, when a torn piece of lined notebook paper floated out of the envelope. I recognized Eliana's handwriting right away—tiny letters, cramped words, remarkably legible, closer to typescript than a human scrawl. "Please call me," the note said, with a phone number. "Love, Eliana."

———

The next day, the police arrested Judith for murdering her husband. "Mob Boss Wife Admits Killing"—lead headline, The Daily News. "She Took an Axe"—front page, The Post. "Wife Confesses to Murder"—page 27, The New York Times. I waited another day, then called Eliana.

We met at Riverside Park, by the playground on 96th Street. I arrived a half hour early. It was a warm, September morning, following a rainy August. Bougainvillea, daisies, dandelions, and tall grasses seemed to burst up right at me as I chose a bench where I could see her coming. She was 20 minutes late. I was about to call when I spotted a familiar walk, straight black hair, now shoulder length, and a neutral expression, with just a hint of a smile, as if she was slightly amused at something, with the emphasis on "slightly." I rose quickly from the bench. "Eliana," I said, and the name emerged involuntarily. I had no intention of saying anything, but the sound came out, unbidden. She nodded, still amused. We didn't touch, no handshake, no hug. She asked if we could take a walk around the park. I wondered if she was referencing our first date, a walk through the streets of Jerusalem. But I didn't ask.

She talked nearly the whole way. She told me what a monster her father had been, her whole life (so much for "he was a saint.") And not just as a crime boss, someone who ordered others killed, who dealt dope, who bribed judges and FBI agents. Eliana gradually learned about all of that, mostly from TV and newspapers, but she never experienced it directly. She spoke about his violent outbursts at home, mostly directed at Judith, but a few times at Eliana.

"Was it, I mean, sexual?" I asked, then immediately regretted the question.

The slight smile returned, as if it were a silly, trivial question. "No, just fists. And kicks. It was enough."

"Of course," I said.

"My mother fought back. She was taller than him, and no pushover. She knew she couldn't call the police—she was in too deep, and he never would have gone along with a divorce. So she hit back. Literally. One time, I wasn't there, she told me about it, they slapped each other so hard, they both ended up bleeding and limping. They shared a taxi to the emergency room. Told the doctor they'd been playing tennis indoors and fell into each other. That's probably the image in my mind that best describes my parents. Riding together in a cab to the hospital, with wounds they gave each other, and coming up with the right lie to keep them out of trouble."

We walked quietly, coming up on Grant's Tomb. Muscle memory urged me to grasp her hand and hold on, but I resisted. "So," I said. "That was it? She'd had enough?" I didn't use the word axe.

She looked at me but didn't answer. We kept walking, around the tomb, then out of the park, up 123rd street toward Broadway. "So, now you see," she said.

See what, I wondered. See why Judith killed Carlos? See why Eliana became such a strange and mesmerizing adult? See why she broke up with me? I just nodded.

She went on, as if she'd sensed my questions. "See why I never talked about my parents. Why I couldn't marry you. I couldn't bring you into that."

I thought about disputing the logic. She couldn't marry me because her father was a mobster? But her parents were "out of the picture." How would they stop her? She couldn't marry me because her parents physically fought all through her childhood? But wouldn't marriage to a relatively sane guy help her heal from those traumas?

But what would be the point in arguing? What was done was done. I was happily married, with a child. I just nodded. She stopped, coincidentally or not, right in front of the Jewish Theological Seminary, where I was ordained, where I spent most of my time away from Eliana that year in New York. She turned to face me. We stood close. Muscle memory, again, this time my face, my lips, my fingers, my legs. She looked into my eyes, half smiling. She was shorter than her mother, shorter than me; she looked up. Those eyes, I thought. God help me. "But now," she said.

═══

The affair lasted six months. How to describe it? It was like being in a foreign country where you know the language so you think you'll be alright, but all the customs, all the assumptions, the looks on people's faces, the smells, the sights, the daily habits—they've all changed, but subtly, almost imperceptibly, so you're shocked one day to realize that you're utterly lost. I learned to lie, not just to Sally, but mostly to Sally. I was surprisingly good at it. I came up with increasingly fanciful excuses—first ritual committee, then adult learning, then choir rehearsal (that raised an eyebrow from my wife, but only because I had no singing talent. Trying to stretch, I told her, and she approved), then long-range planning, finance and then I started making up names for committees: the spirituality committee, the progressive education committee, political action, innovation committee. Suddenly our staid, traditional synagogue became a hotbed of new, interesting ideas, but only in my lies. Of course, I had to lie to Rabbi Marmelstein, the senior rabbi, to explain why I was suddenly unavailable several nights a week. Asthma, I told him. A chronic curse, episodic, seasonal. Doctor's order: Rest a little more until the flare-up passes, probably in the winter when the cold weather kills the allergens. He nodded sagely. Sage nods were one of his specialties.

It would be inaccurate to say I felt guilty. Rather, guilt became an all-compassing reality, like skin, tactile, tight, pervasive. Everything provoked guilt: what I ate for breakfast, leading daily services, reading novels, walking Molly to daycare, riding the subway, napping, waking up. I learned something fantastic and devastating about love. I loved Sally. I had no interest in a divorce. I was in love with her. But I fell for Eliana, or better stumbled and crashed in love, and then kept falling, waiting to hit bottom. Sensory phenomena conquered my mind, intoxicated me, made me stupid: the distinctly different odors of the two women I slept with, the strangely different feel of their skin, the pounding heat of the shower in Eliana's midtown apartment, fatigue from many nights without sleep. It had to end, I knew, but I made no effort to end it, couldn't imagine it ending, begged God that it last forever.

It didn't. We got caught. It happened during our first and only weekend getaway together. Surprisingly, it wasn't the ridiculous lie I told Sally—a young rabbis' retreat in the Hamptons, easily refutable; rabbis would never get together over a weekend, that's when we work hardest. Rather, it was a strange coincidence. Eliana's parents owned a mansion in Montauk. Carlos, of course, was acutely sensitive to security, so the home was set far back from the winding single-lane road, and surrounded by a thick forest of trees. The closest neighbors were half a mile away; Eliana had never met them, didn't know their names, knew nothing about them. I knew them. They knew me.

We were snowshoeing. A sudden, late February blizzard hit on Friday night. We woke to eight inches of snow and an unplowed driveway and road. Eliana suggested cross country skiing, but I pointed to the weird tennis-racket-like shoes hanging on a peg in the garage—snowshoes. Eliana's weird half smile expanded into almost a grin. "That's my favorite," she said.

I could see why. She found a pair my size—I shared a shoe size with Carlos—and we walked straight out the back door onto a steep snowy hill. It was like navigating an environment with different rules of gravity. The shoes sunk into the white fluff, but then came up easily, as if the snow was water, or air. Rabbits and squirrels hopped along the surface of the snow. Birds sang, an odd soundtrack to a winter wonderland. Clumps of dazzling white snow still clung to the oak branches, along with gleaming silver icicles, but the air was warming, so the icicles melted into fabulous, unworldly shapes. It was glorious. There were no people.

Until there were. At first, with the sun in my eyes, I mistook them for midsize mammals, maybe mountain goats or bobcats. By the time they moved closer and Eliana's tall, woolen hat blocked the glare, it was too late; they recognized me. "Rabbi Greenberg?" the man asked. It was Judah Loeb, a lawyer at Marcus and Haas, a prestigious Midtown firm. His arm muscles bulged through his dark blue, Gore-Tex sweater, and his chest heaved forward, like he was about to bump me. He was easy to recognize; he was short, a good six inches shorter than I, but ripped into sharp angles and a bulging six pack. Judah was one of the few congregational leaders even close to my age, probably five years older. He'd been on the search committee that brought me to the synagogue. After my first interview, he dragged me to a packed Knicks game at Madison Square Garden. I drank two beers and pretended to love basketball. Sally and I had been to his apartment twice, once an elegant dinner for just the four of us, the other a fundraiser for one of his law partners who was running for Congress. I remembered Sally and his wife Joanne retreating to a corner of the living room, giggling like old friends. Judah removed his sunglass, grinned, and took in the site: me; a strange and a beautiful companion, not my wife; virgin snow; a crystal forest. But Joanne looked only at Eliana. "Where's Sally?" she asked, still staring at Eliana, as if addressing the question to her.

"Um," I said. I watched my breath move toward Joanne. Eliana moved slightly, so she was standing behind me, as if protecting herself from Joanne's relentless gaze. I tried to remember if Sally had a connection to Joanne independent of me. "She couldn't come."

"On call?" she asked.

"Yes," I said, and immediately remembered. Joanne interned at the same hospital as Sally. They knew each other well.

Well enough that she knew Sally wasn't on call that weekend. Evidence of a lie, which meant evidence of a guilty conscience, which, in an astonishingly short amount of time—on the Tuesday after the fateful Saturday in the snow—meant Sally kicking me out of the apartment after slapping me hard on the face. Two days later, I got fired.

I moved in with Andy, who immediately gave me a job supervising the ritual purification of dead bodies. After three months of soapy, disinfectant smells, psalms and naked corpses, he fired me, but only because he arranged an interview with *Hevruta*, a national Jewish adult education outfit that Andy's family funded. "You can't get back together with Sally if you're working with dead folks all day," he explained. "No offense."

"Who says I'm getting back together with Sally?"

He shrugged. We were in the body purification room, dressing a corpse in white cotton garments. Andy adjusted the head-covering, smoothed out the wrinkles from the shirt and pants, and took a half step back to inspect our handiwork. "Perfect," he said, and he could have been complimenting a new bride on her beautiful gown, or a teenage son on his way to the prom. "Can you believe how good this guy looks?" he asked me. "Flat belly, full head of black hair. No skin cancers, good teeth. If it weren't for the fact that he's dead, I'd say he was in perfect health."

"Andy," I said.

"She calls me every once in a while," Andy said, flicking non-existent lint from the shirt. "Asks about you. I made a few suggestions. Least I could do. I was the one who hooked you up with that mob family."

Sally texted me the next day. I got the new job. She forgave me.

I didn't contact Eliana at all after the disaster in the snow. She called twice in six months, and both times I let it go to voicemail, then deleted her message. My last communication from her was a New

York Times article she forwarded to me—without comment—of her mother's sentencing: 99 years. I immediately deleted the email, and didn't read the article. Because I'd already read it, in addition to articles in the Post, the Daily News, The Observer, CNN, and the Drudge Report. I still Googled Eliana, at first once a week, but I managed to cut back to once a month, and then every once in a while. When the spirit moved me. When I'd hear a particular song. When a sunbeam would hit me at a certain angle. When I fucking felt like it. Just to see her picture. Just to remember.

April, 2020

I wasn't surprised that Eliana at 42 looked nearly identical to Eliana at 30, or 25. I'd seen a recent picture—a half-smiling Eliana, black hair flowing past her shoulders, twinkling brown eyes that suggested sadness, or wisdom, or wisdom born of sadness (which I now knew was a misimpression), high cheekbones, thin fingers. She was handing one of those fake gigantic checks to the grateful headmaster of a Jewish day school in Riverdale. Eliana had become a philanthropist, parleying Carlos' crime fortune into a well-heeled and extremely generous family foundation that she ran. A colleague of mine once told me there was over a billion dollars in the endowment, which meant grants totaling millions of dollars a year, and at least a third went to Jewish causes. Every once in a while, her name would come up at Hevruta, where I was now development director—Hey, shouldn't we hit up the Klein Foundation? "Not interested in adult learning," I'd immediately say. Which was true. Eliana's foundation avoided my chosen field.

But now, here she was, maskless, a socially distant six feet away, chuckling her humorless chuckle.

"Strange coincidence," I said. "Judith here. The three of us in the same county, within five miles of each other."

"Coincidence?"

"You think it's on purpose? That I'm stalking your mother?"

She tilted her head, taking me in. I tried to remember if I lied to her as much as I'd lied to Sally. Had I given her multiple reasons to disbelieve me, to question her trust in me? Probably. "No," she said. "I don't think you're stalking her. But I'm afraid she might be stalking you. She requested the transfer to this particular prison."

I looked around. The park still wasn't empty. I spotted one young couple jogging together, three women pushing strollers, and an elderly couple out for a walk around the neighborhood. But everyone kept their distance. Oddly, that included not meeting each other's eyes, as if the virus could be transmitted through line of site. I had the strange thought that it was unfortunate our extramarital affair hadn't happened during a plague. Maybe we wouldn't have gotten caught. "You think she requested a transfer because I live here? Isn't that sort of farfetched? Maybe it's just a more comfortable prison. I mean, does she even remember me?"

"Apparently she does."

"What do you mean?"

"She asked me to find you. She wants to see you."

Was this a practical joke? A dream? A set-up? Was she wearing a wire? I stared at her. The half-smile had disappeared, but she looked unfazed, her head slightly tilted, studying me. She brushed black hair from her forehead.

"*See* me?" I said. "Like, in person? Are you out of your mind?"

"It's just up the road," she said, casually, as if she were just asking me to pick up sanitary wipes at the pharmacy.

"It's a pandemic! In a prison."

"Oh, they're very careful. They'll set up a meeting for the two of you on the grounds. At a table, six feet apart, like we're meeting now. Our lawyers worked it out."

"Eliana, still, it's totally inappropriate. Not to mention dangerous. And I don't see . . . "

"She said you owe it to her. I sort of agree."

I shook my head, then watched the joggers, wondered who they were. "Owe it to her?"

"That's our feeling." She put a card on the picnic table halfway between us. "The prison social worker," she said. "She'll arrange the meeting."

I stared at the card, making no move to pick it up. Eliana watched me with a blank expression, eyes nearly closed, lips tightly pursed, her hands in her lap, folded into fists. It was her guarded self, the persona she shrank into to avoid emotion or confrontation. I recognized the look from whenever I brought up her parents, or asked about her childhood. I knew there was no breaking through without changing the subject. I waited a good five minutes before talking. Eliana barley moved, keeping her half-closed eyes fixed on me. "Just text me the contact information," I said. I wasn't going to touch that card.

She took out her phone. I hesitated for a second before giving her my number, but I did. She thumbed in the text, got up and quickly walked away. I thought about following her. I was suddenly insanely curious about where a billionaire might live in Northampton. But she was walking quickly, and the conversation had exhausted me.

The next day I visited the prison. It was, as Eliana pointed out, "just down the road," or really just up the hill, less than five miles from the center of town. The impression, as I pulled into the complex, was more of a college dormitory at an all-girls school than a county jail. I'd been there a few times, a favor for the local congregational rabbi who had no interest in visiting convicts. The last time I was there, I'd seen inmates and guards tossing frisbees on a wide front lawn. Once, in the winter, I saw prisoners sliding down a snowy hill on sleds made from cardboard boxes. Of course, there were armed guards, and a guard tower, and barbed wire. And inside, in addition to a brightly lit, well-stocked library and clean classrooms, were tiny cells, brawny CO's and punishment rooms. So more like a girls college in hell.

This time I wouldn't be going inside at all. Eliana's wealth clearly bought her mother special privileges. A masked social worker met me at the entrance to the parking lot. She pantomimed me to follow her, and we walked single file, me a good 10 feet behind her. She led me to a wooden picnic table, remarkably similar to the one at Childe's Park where I'd met with Eliana. She pointed me to sit down, again a pantomime, as if sign language had become a new form of social distancing. I smiled at her, but then realized I was also wearing a mask, and she wouldn't be able see my facial expressions. "Thank you," I said through my mask, and it felt like I was breaking a taboo by speaking. She nodded and walked away quickly. Twenty minutes later a tall, armed, surgically masked male guard stepped out of the closest building, followed, at a six-foot distance, by Judith, and then, six feet later, by an even taller guard, who'd wrapped the entirety of his face except for his eyes in a black bandana. The two guards moved to a safe distance facing the picnic table, and Judith sat down across from me.

She touched her white, disposable mask. "Do you mind if I take this off?" she asked.

"I think you should keep it on," I said quickly. I looked at the guards. Wasn't that the rule? Wouldn't they enforce it? I was about to walk away when she took her hands off her mask.

"I think I'm going to be sick," she said.

"What!"

"No, no, Peter. You need to calm down. Not that kind of sick. It's just looking at you. Remembering those terrible days. You remember, don't you?"

I watched her brown eyes, so similar to Eliana's. With the rest of her face masked, it was her only kinetic feature, the only non-verbal clue to how she felt being with me. I wondered if I'd see the ball-bearing tears. Her hair had turned stringy and silvery black, and it was tied back in a ponytail. She wore blue crocks and an orange jumpsuit, a size or two too small; her ankles peaked through the bottom and her breasts and elbows bulged through the top, as if she were wearing a comfortable straight jacket.

"I remember," I said.

"Of course you do."

I waited. She fidgeted, scratched her arms, adjusted her mask, twisted her hairband, all the while meeting my gaze with her brown eyes. She'd asked to see me, so it seemed reasonable and fair to let her speak first. But the silence was deeply disconcerting, and anyway I wanted to get out of there as soon as possible, so I talked. "You asked to see me?"

"Yes," she said.

I nodded, waited. "And?" I said.

"I'd like you to speak with Eliana."

I smiled, then quickly realized that of course she couldn't see my lips, so I faked a laugh. "I spoke with her. She said you needed to speak with me."

"Yes." She fiddled with her mask.

"Judith."

"I needed to speak with you to tell you to speak with Eliana."

Riddles, I thought. Games. A familiar feeling washed over me—that Judith and Eliana were not real, were figments of a scriptwriter's imagination. It was a particularly fantastic form of denial. I'm just a small-town rabbi, a bureaucrat at a mostly insignificant organization. Organized crime, murder, adultery—these things are fictions, alien to my dull life, except as entertaining diversions. But I took in the surroundings, watched the masked, uniformed guards play with their phones, noted the barbed-wire fence not more than 20 feet away. The feeling faded; this was real. Anyway, I solved the riddle, and it wasn't really much of a riddle at all. Certainly not a game. I sighed through my mask, misting up my glasses. "I'll talk to her," I said.

The social worker intercepted me halfway down the path to the parking lot. She called to me from six feet away. "Will you be coming back, Rabbi Greenberg?" she asked. Had I told her I was a rabbi? My name? Did I know her? So hard to tell with masks. "Probably not," I said. Her eyes drooped slightly. Disappointment? I didn't inquire further, didn't wait to find out. I hurried to my car.

———

"She said I should talk to you. She wanted to talk to me to tell me to talk to you. If that makes any sense." I called Eliana the day after my visit. I didn't want to risk another in person encounter, and anyway I doubted she'd want to see me again.

"Of course, it makes sense," she said quickly. I marveled at the cool anger, the spiky irritation in her voice. It was, in fact, the normal way she spoke to most people, most of the time. For me, long ago, that low, chilly tone was part of her allure, her mystery. But it wasn't how she spoke with me when we were sleeping together. Intimacy melted the ice. But now the ice was back. "We both know what she means," she said.

"We do?"

"Oh, come on."

"Okay," I said. I felt a chill. "Well, should we talk about it?"

She hung up. A minute later she texted me. "Call me tomorrow," she wrote. "Same time."

I didn't. Instead I took a walk around the neighborhood, my third walk of the day. The twins led the way, crisscrossing down the empty street in their silver scooters; Molly stayed home with Jacob. As we cut through the dirt path toward Mason's Creek, I reviewed in my mind the details of that afternoon in Manhattan. Did it really happen?

September, 2007

It was the third time that I'd slept with Eliana after the funeral. No longer a fling, too early for a midlife crisis, this was now nothing more than what it seemed, adultery, an affair, a betrayal. We'd both dozed off on Eliana's king-size bed in her Midtown apartment. She woke me up by staring at me. I jerked awake, feeling watched. She half-smiled at me. I gathered up some courage, and asked about the scars on her wrists, inner thigh and back.

She fingered the one on her wrist, a tiny divot in the flesh, only half a dime's length, certainly not a suicide attempt, unless she'd rapidly changed her mind. "You never noticed before?" she asked. "When we were together?"

Had I? I wasn't the most observant guy back then, and in bed the stark fact of her glorious nakedness would have overwhelmed any other body observations. But there was an obvious reason why I was noticing now. "Your father?" I said, thinking of Carlos with Judith.

She nodded.

"When you were young?" I asked. "What ages?"

She flashed a full, sad smile, the sudden dampness in her eyes warming her expression. "All ages," she said. "Every year of my life. Until he died."

She took me on a grisly tour. First her left thumb, a splash of ugly black on the bottom half of the nail. "When he closed the car door on my hand. It never healed." Dots of fading scars under both arms—cigarette burns. Red lines under both breasts—fingernail scratches. Blotches on both knees from when he shoved her down the stairs. Blackened toenail from a stomping boot.

"Did he ever . . . ?"

She shook her head and said nothing. No, or she couldn't talk about it? I didn't press. I fingered the scars on her right knee, waited for her to continue.

"He wasn't going to stop."

"No," I said.

"He wouldn't."

I touched the palm of her hand. She clenched her fist around my finger. "So you can see why," she said.

Again? I thought. Something I'm supposed to see. But I wasn't going to guess. "Why what?"

She kissed my cheek, released my fingers. "Why I had to kill him."

━━━

She'd found the axe at the Montauk mansion, for splitting logs, or, as she remembered from when she was 6, threatening her mother. She assumed murdering her father would be the easiest crime in the world to get away with. Suspicion would immediately fall on his fellow crime bosses. She'd read in one of her favorite mystery novels that mobsters often make a statement when killing informers—beat the victim to death with a baseball bat, or burn him alive with gasoline. She'd planned to show up for dinner on a night when the blond girlfriend was visiting her sister, drug him with a drink, then slice off his head while he slept. Instead, she spotted him sneaking a cigarette in the alley behind the building and attacked from behind. "It only took one swing," she told me, still caressing my hand, like she was telling me a bedtime story. "I was aiming for the neck, but he ducked, and I smashed in his skull. He died right away."

The problem was the crime novel turned out to be just that, a novel, a fiction. Mobsters didn't execute each other with axes; in fact, the axe proved just the opposite, a crime of passion, an amateur, not a professional. And with Carlos' history of beating her up, she assumed she'd be a suspect, especially since, despite her caution and her pedigree, she was an inexperienced murderer. She was sure she left some clue behind.

Her mother figured it out right away. If it wasn't a mob killing, that really left only two suspects, and she knew she didn't do it. At first, she insisted that Eliana leave the country. But she didn't want a life on the lam for her daughter, and besides, all the decent countries had extradition treaties. Cuba was out of the question; they'd confiscate her wealth and then expel her. In the end, she decided to take the blame. It was my fault he terrorized you all those years, she told her daughter. I married him. I stayed with him. I knew who he was, what he was doing to you. Eliana gave Judith the murder weapon so she could cover it with her own fingerprints. She confessed two days after the funeral, one day before I called Eliana, and we embarked on our illicit affair.

The problem was now, in jail, facing decades locked behind prison walls, Judith was having second thoughts. "Maybe you could help," Eliana told me, naked, scarred, in bed, speaking softly, caressing me. "Visit her. Talk to her. Help her think things through."

That was the first time I visited a prison, the Metropolitan Corrections Center in Lower Manhattan. That time it meant triggering three metal detector alarms, for no reason I could imagine—I'd stripped off my belt, deposited my cell phone, wore sneakers. Then I endured three full-body pat downs, and waited over an hour for them to find Judith. It was impossible to set appointments or to phone ahead. The winding hallways reeked of disinfectant. Doors slammed shut with a metallic clang. Prisoners cackled and screamed. This was no college dorm.

I'd told them I was Judith's rabbi, but they treated me like I was her attorney, with a private visitor's room—a tiny, windowless 6 x 6 cell with two battered elementary school desks, with swear words and pornographic images carved into the wood. A tall, muscular, male guard, reeking of tobacco, led me to the cell, gestured for me to sit, then left without a word. The door closed with a loud click. I wondered if I was locked in. I thought for a moment about claustrophobia, of prison rape, but the door quickly swung open. A thin, wiry female guard, nearly a foot shorter than me, led Judith into the cell. With a thick Queens accent, she told me to bang on the door when I was through.

In those days, Judith and Eliana looked very much alike. Same shoulder-length black hair, same brown eyes, same Mona Lisa smile on thin lips, same clear skin, a similar air of mystery and beauty. I wondered why I hadn't noticed the resemblance when I first met Judith, at Andy's funeral parlor. I noticed it now.

"Hello Peter," she said, and her voice was different than her daughter's. Unless she was speaking to an intimate, Eliana's speech was robotic, flat and clear, as if she were giving precise driving directions to a stranger. Judith's voice, musical, warm, bell-like, always sounded like it was aimed at a friend or a family member or a lover. "I think I know why you're here." She looked around the room. There wasn't much to see. The two of us. The ancient desks with the pornographic graffiti. The white walls, streaked with yellow from some unknown substance. A single, bare bulb. She felt under her desk, then mine; looked up and studied the bulb. "We have to be careful," she said. "I know you talked to Eliana. So, I'll just ask you a question. Would you do it, for your daughter?"

"Admit to murder so she'd get off?"

She exhaled, shook her head, pointed to the bulb. A hidden mic? How could I possibly know? In retrospect, it's amazing how ill-suited I was for all this—adultery, deception, crime, conspiracy. And yet I kept doing it. "Sorry," I said. I thought for a moment. "I can't answer. It's too hypothetical. I can't imagine myself in your situation."

She glared at me. "Peter, why did you come here?"

"Eliana. She told me . . . "

"Never mind," she snapped. "Just answer my question! Would you do it?"

I looked at the door. Could they hear her? Would they burst in if she attacked me? I pictured Molly, my 3-year-old. That morning, I'd left her splashing with delight in our tiny kid pool on the balcony, chanting random rhymes in a melody she composed on the spot: fish, dish, wish, swish. Supremely precious, supremely vulnerable. Would I do it? What wouldn't I do to protect her? "Yes," I said.

She nodded, suddenly calm. A single ball-bearing tear escaped her left eye. She brushed it way, as if it were an insect. "Okay," she said. "Okay. One more question, Rabbi Peter. Are you sleeping with my daughter?"

Was this a trap? Had Sally, or the president of the congregation, set this visit up to entrap me, trick me into confessing my guilt? It's funny how paranoia seizes you when you're already in trouble. "No," I lied. "I'm not sleeping with Eliana. She's just an old friend."

She kept her eye on me, watched me closely, but reached over to knock sharply on the door. Two guards entered immediately, one to take her back to her cell, the other to accompany me out of the jail. I set off two metal detectors on my way out.

April, 2020

Ten years later, while the boys circled the lake on their silver scooters, veering off to a safe distance whenever a human approached, I contemplated that lie. I didn't want Judith to think I was biased, that I was only advising her to accept a lifetime in jail because I was in love again with her daughter. Also, I instinctively lied about the affair, lying about it came so naturally that it began to seem like the truth.

Also, I didn't want Eliana going to jail, even after she admitting to axing her father. It's not that I was thinking of a future life with her, of divorce, remarriage, a new family. In my limited experience, extramarital affairs obstructed thoughts of the future, like a shade tree blocks the sun. Future meant measured planning, meant consequences, meant complex, multi-layered, unimaginable pain. Future meant imagining that pain, in detail. During the affair, I fled thoughts of the future, and lived only for the next encounter. Lying to Judith while she considered a life in prison wasn't part of a scheme to win Eliana. It was just an instinctive gesture to keep things going for as long as they could.

It was also a big enough sin that, out of guilt, I risked disease to visit her in prison. Ultimately that same guilt nudged me to call Eliana while the boys skipped stones into the lake. I agreed to meet her at her house. She texted me the address. I herded the boys back home, then walked the wooded, mostly empty streets to Northampton's one recognizably ritzy neighborhood.

As it turned out, I'd been in the house. Years before a young couple who created a mega-successful comic book franchise built the mansion, modeling it, according to rumor, on Hogwarts, though to me it looked more like the house on the Munsters, with towers, spires, gables, belfries and a 50-square-yard bush maze on the front lawn. It was undeniably swanky, but also spooky, with its cobalt gray paint job, and the sense, probably an optical illusion, that the towers were leaning out, threatening anyone who approached. The multi-millionaire couple were friends of friends—Northampton's a small town—so they invited me to a cocktail party raising money for a local comic book museum. They'd decorated the place with garish, multi-colored superhero art: DC—Superman, Batman, etc . . . – on the grounds outside, and Marvel—Spidey, The Fantastic Four, the Silver Surfer—on the inside. I got a splitting headache minutes after I arrived, so I fled.

Apparently so had they, and sold their haunted house to Eliana. It figures, I thought. The most expensive home in Northampton, and the weirdest. That's what she would buy.

She opened the door, quickly retreated six feet, then gestured for me to come in. Eliana had always been a difficult person to read, but now, with a homemade yellow polka-dotted bandana mask that covered her face from the top of her nose on down, it was nearly impossible. But I thought I detected some warmth in her eyes, or at least a thawing from when I'd last seen her. I wondered why she was so angry at me. She, after all, had broken up with me the first time, and the second time, it was the circumstances.

She led me through a wide corridor with Teenage Mutant Ninja Turtles painted directly on the walls, past a concert hall equipped with a grand piano, to the patio. We sat on opposite sides of a glass table, right next to the infinity pool. I watched the waters trail down a hill. She took off her mask. I shrugged and took off mine.

"She told me to talk to you," I said.

"I know." She looked at her lap.

"I think I know what we're supposed to talk about. Do you?"

She exhaled slowly, didn't meet my eye. Then nodded. "She wants you to talk me into turning myself in. To confess." She looked at me, waited for my arguments.

"I have no intention of trying to talk you into anything. It's not my role. Not my job."

She nodded. "Okay. But maybe just tell me what you think?"

What was it with these two women, this mother-daughter pair, that craved my opinion on the most important decisions they faced? I'd given up congregation life a long time ago. Literally no one sought my opinion now on deeply personal matters, including my wife and children. But somehow a spark of rabbinic wisdom lingered on me like an odor when facing Judith or Eliana.

I remained silent, so she pressed me. "What would you do?" she asked. "You answered the question for her. Answer it for me."

I watched her brown eyes blink back normal shaped tears. I thought of Sally, of the kids. Without thinking, I leaned forward, into her space. "I'd confess," I said. "Face the consequences." I shrugged. "You had your reasons. I imagine the judge would be lenient."

She nodded several times, her head bobbing like a toy doll. "I'll do it," she said softly. It sounded like a religious oath, like a nervous naïve bride assenting to an arranged marriage. She leaned across the table. Our faces were now inches away. "Can I show you the rest of the house?" We walked past the Ninja Turtles into one of the bedrooms.

The next morning, back home, I woke up with a splitting headache and a fever of 103. I slept most of the day. Sally brought me soup and we agreed I wouldn't leave the bedroom. The next morning the fever was up to 104 and I was too dizzy to stand. I couldn't sleep, couldn't eat, couldn't get warm despite the high fever. I asked Sally for more blankets. I shivered madly, then sweated then shivered then sweated in an unholy cycle of suffering. No respiratory symptoms, I thought, with relief. Then, as if in response, I coughed eight times in rapid succession like a machine gun, then wheezed, and coughed again, wet coughs filled with phlegm, that nevertheless felt like dry coughs, like pieces of my lungs were shaking free. The pain in my chest was indescribable. Sally drove me to an outdoor testing station next to Cooley Dickinson hospital. I shoved a swab up my nose. The doctor listened to my chest, studied my tongue, seemed to think things over, and sent me home. She called the next day to tell me the test was positive. Any trouble breathing? I coughed four times. "No," I said. She laughed. "Drink lots of water. And tell Sally to bring you in right away if the coughing gets worse."

My fever hovered between 102 and 104 the next week. The hallucinations started the fourth day. I saw Marlon Brando standing next to my bed, but it wasn't Marlon Brando, it was the Godfather, the character he played. He recruited me; I became a hitman. A half hour later it was Stringer Bell, the drug lord from The Wire, selling me heroin. I asked Sally what he was doing here. Didn't he live in Baltimore? And, come to think of it, wasn't he dead, murdered by Omar? I lost 20 pounds. My daily diet, left outside the door by Sally or Molly, was water, a half piece of dried toast and a mug of chicken soup. I coughed through the nights, spitting up gobs of phlegm. I was too dizzy to read, to watch TV, to check my phone, to engage in conversation. Sitting up in bed was my daily chore; sometimes I succeeded, sometimes not. Then I got better. I woke up one day with no fever. I stood up, walked slowly to the bathroom, brushed my teeth and shaved. Then the shivering restarted, violent, uncontrollable. I fell against the cool, blue-tiled wall, fought hard to avoid passing out and collapsing on the floor. I barely made it back to the bed. The fever spiked, back to 103.

But that was the beginning of the end. For the next week I'd wake up almost normal, just some lingering fuzz in my brain, a slight tickle in the chest, and mutter "Thank God." But after two or three or four or six or eight hours, the monster would rush back hurling me into bed, at the mercy of the chills, the steady coughing, the hallucinations. Finally, a day without fever. Then another, also without a headache. The coughing fits ended. Then three days without fever, then four. I got dressed walked into the kitchen. Molly was stirring soup. She recoiled when she saw me, backed up three feet, and grabbed a mask out of her jeans pocket. "I'm better," I said, and walked into the back yard. The sun hung high in the sky. It was May 1. Three hummingbirds hovered over a feeder. I shielded my eyes from the glare and watched two squirrels race up our loquat tree. My phone buzzed.

"Welcome back," Sally said.

"Good to be back."

"We need to talk."

I pondered that. "Right now?"

"When I get home. Soon."

I hovered my hand over the phone for a few seconds, then decided. I punched in Eliana's number. Voicemail picked up right away, a computer message. I tried again. Same message, anonymous, metallic. Could have been Eliana, I thought, mimicking a computer. I thumbed off the phone, and switched to text, thought about what to write. I looked up, searching the trees for words, and there was Sally, in her turquoise scrubs leaning against the glass door, at least twice as far away as recommended.

"Why didn't you just tell me?" she asked.

Tell her? About Eliana? About Judith? That I'd lost my mind, as well as any ethical pretense? Her words sounded harsh, accusing, but a surgical mask covered her face, so I couldn't read her expression.

"Do you need the mask?" I asked her softly.

She chuckled, peeled it off. "Sorry," she said. "Just used to wearing it all day in the hospital." She smiled. "Why didn't you tell me?"

"Tell you what?"

"That you'd visited the prison. If you'd told me beforehand, I could have gone over some better safety precautions. Or better yet, talked you out of going. That's probably how you caught it."

The unspoken assumption in our house had been that I'd caught it from her, that she had the disease but was asymptomatic. She, after all, spent her days at a hospital that serviced dozens of Covid patients a day. We were social distancing in our shambling house, but a single careless touch of a single doorknob or washing machine dial or a brush against the wall could have infected me.

"There was a Jewish prisoner. She wanted to see a rabbi. We took, well, they took precautions. Masks for everyone. Lots of hand sanitizer. Sinks. Soap and water. Everyone kept six feet away, at least."

She nodded. "Yeah, that's what Marla told me. A lot of prisons are becoming hot zones, but not this one. Better leadership. More room."

"Marla?" I said.

"The social worker. The one who met you, took you to your prisoner. She works part time at the hospital and part time at the jail. She told me she saw you. She was grateful and impressed. It's almost impossible now to get clergy to visit prisons. She said you were very brave. But you're not going back, are you? We don't know if you're immune. At this point, it would just be stupid."

Was this it? Of all my sins, I'm only getting caught on this one? Is that really how the world works? "No," I said "I won't be going back. "That prisoner, I think they'll be freeing her pretty soon."

"Who was it?" Curious, not accusing. At least that's how she sounded.

My heart raced. I felt a cough coming. I lifted my elbow to cover my mouth; Sally recoiled, but nothing emerged from my lungs. I was feeling healthier by the minute. "Marla didn't tell you?"

She shook her head. "Confidentiality. It's just as strict with social workers as it is with doctors. Was it someone you knew?"

I nodded. "I'd met her years ago. I don't really know her well."

She looked at me, waiting further explanation.

"In New York," I said.

Then the twins burst through the screen door, excited to see their mother in the middle of the day, and their father upright and released from his prison cell bedroom. Molly and Jacob joined us, hand in hand—a glorious family reunion. It didn't last long. Mom had to go back to work.

Later that evening, I got a text from an unknown number. It was a link to a Daily News piece with the headline, "Axe Murderer Back at Rikers." The short, two-paragraph article described how Judith Klein Epstein, "convicted murderer of her mob-boss spouse," had been transferred from a cushy county prison in Western Massachusetts to a high-security penitentiary in New York. Spokespersons from both prisons offered no comment. I phoned the unknown text number and was immediately sent to voicemail. No greeting, no robotic voice, no voice at all, just a buzz. I hung up.

Two days later, fully recovered, on a neighborhood walk with all four kids—Jacob had stopped accosting folks on the street—I got another text from a different unknown number—again a link to an article, this one from The Post. "Mobster's Sister Hangs Herself." It was Ida, Carlos' sister, Eliana's aunt, who'd openly accused Judith of murdering her saintly brother. Police offered no motive as to why a well-off 74-year-old woman would kill herself. A family spokesperson had no comment. "We request that you honor the family's need for privacy."

For two weeks, I called both numbers repeatedly, along with the other number I had for Eliana. Always a greeting-less voicemail. By the second week, the numbers were not in service. Emails bounced back. One day I biked to her haunted house and banged on the heavy door. No answer. A For Sale sign was stuck on the front lawn, next to the maze. Eliana was in the wind.

March 2023

Back to normal! Which is to say everyone else in the family went back to normal. Sally resumed a regular radiologist schedule, 4 days a week, one weekend a month. Molly gratefully fled back to Wesleyan, the twins returned to middle school, and Jacob, still the friendliest of us, started kindergarten. Northampton's downtown street life—the restaurants, cafes, street musicians, clubs—resumed slowly at first, but then with zest, though also with a residue of anxiety, naked fear, and loss. Fewer hugs. Almost no handshakes. And, if not six feet, still distancing, even if it was only six inches. It was not at all unusual to see a pedestrian or two wearing a mask. Joggers continued to sidestep each other by at least 20 feet. Neighbors avoided each other's eyes, a remnant of the primal fear that danger travels through the force of a gaze.

My habits didn't change all that much. I continued to work from home, but now commuted much less to Boston. With the recession, the agency cut my hours, so I was only working half-time, mostly writing grants. I was in the middle of scouring the web for new Jewish or education foundations when my boss, the executive director phoned.

"We've got to try the Klein Foundation. I'm reading about them every day. Apparently, they've shifted their mission. Their goal is to get the whole Jewish non-profit sector through the recession. They are ridiculously well endowed. I think Eliana Klein is trying to spend down all the money. And, Peter, it's billions."

"They don't fund . . . "

"You're not listening. That excuse doesn't work anymore. They'll fund any Jewish agency now. We just have to make a case. Look, this could get you back to full time."

"Okay."

"I'm not hearing a lot of enthusiasm. You know I didn't want to bring this up. But is this personal? I heard a rumor that you dated Eliana Klein back in the day."

No point in lying. The first time we were entirely out in the open. "That's true," I admitted.

"Call her, Peter. Desperate times, you know."

I waited a beat. "Do you know where her money comes from?"

"Oh please. Spare me the rumors. Hospitals take her money. Homeless shelters. We're too good for it?"

I sighed. "I'll call."

After Eliana erased her Northampton existence she moved back to Manhattan. I kept track of her through Jewish social media. She never contacted me, and I'd had enough of trying to reach her. But now my job depended on it, so I went to the foundation website, downloaded the 15-page application and spent a week, full time, filling it out. Instead of sending it in, I called the office number, expecting voicemail. But an intern picked up, and told me she'd be happy to answer any questions after I submitted all the required forms.

"I was thinking I could bring it in, in person," I said.

"Uh, sure," she said. "I'm here 8:30 to 5. You can leave it on my desk if I'm out."

"No, I meant in person to Eliana."

"Oh no, she doesn't . . . "

"I'm an old friend. Maybe, could you ask?"

"I don't think . . . "

"Just ask." I reminded her of my name.

"Hold on a second," she said. I stayed on hold for 20 minutes. Loud klezmer music blared through the phone, cycling through the same bluesy clarinet tune. I remembered that Eliana despised klezmer. Finally, the intern returned. "She'll see you tomorrow," she said. "7 AM."

———

She sat behind the biggest desk I'd ever seen, black, shiny, sharp, threatening angles and edges, more tank than workspace. At least 10 feet long and maybe that wide, the leather chair she sat in too distant from the front of the desk to reach out a hand to shake, not that either of us offered a hand. Oddly, there were no visitor chairs in the room, only a plush tan sofa and matching love seat. She didn't rise when I walked in, just pointed me to the couch. Then she got up. I was afraid she was going to sit down next to me, but she only moved to a corner of the desk with a raised platform meant for standing.

"You're here to talk about my mother?" I shouldn't have been surprised that she looked exactly the same. It had been less than two years. Those many months had turned my hair almost completely gray, but Eliana somehow kept her youthful beauty from 25 to 30 to 45. If anything, she looked better, less frail, more confident.

"I've got an application," I told her, holding up my briefcase as if she'd asked to inspect it for contraband.

"Okay," she said. She waited.

"And I'd like to talk about your mother. And Ida. And your father."

She smiled. Half smiled. It was her reserved face, her masked face that revealed nothing.

"How much are you asking for?" she said.

"You sent me the story about Ida's suicide to intimidate me. Really, it was a threat. If I go to the police, that could happen to me."

"You know, we normally don't fund adult learning. We don't see the value, especially when compared to early childhood interventions, or fourth-grade literacy, or anti-poverty campaigns, or global warming."

"Also, you could always blackmail me. There was the affair after the funeral. But that was already public record, and Sally knew all about it. So you had to get me to sleep with you in Northampton. Of course, I went along, eagerly. But for you, I think it was part of your scheme. Another reason for me to shut up."

"But now we're making an exception. All legitimate Jewish agencies deserve a chance to survive the pandemic. So we've changed out guidelines. Temporarily."

She thinks I'm wearing a wire, I thought. Or maybe she's recording this. "I thought I knew you," I said. "I guess I didn't. You killed Ida. You had your mother sent back to a plague-infested hellhole. You used me to set up your mother. And you slept with me just to keep me quiet. You're ruthless. And relentless."

She looked down at me and tilted her head, as if she were receiving some manner of communication. "No," she said. "You're right. You didn't know me. You don't." She fingered her wrist. I thought of bruises, her body scars, the night she took me on a tour of her wounds.

I nodded. "I should have tried harder," I said.

"Yes," she said. We watched each other—a staring contest. I won; she looked away, at my briefcase. "You can leave the application with me."

=====

On the train ride home, my boss called. "What the hell happened there?" she asked.

"What do you mean?" I said. I looked out the window at the Connecticut shore. "You heard back already?"

"They wired the money. It's in the bank."

"How much?" I asked."

"Thirty-six dollars."

"Thirty. Thirty-six. Did you say thirty-six *dollars*?" We'd asked for half a million.

"Yep. Listen Peter, call me when you get back to Northampton. We have to rethink your position."

I arrived home in time for dinner—the twins grilled Beyond Burgers; Sally made potato salad. But I waited until late evening to call. Sally snored softly, which meant she was sound asleep. Jacob tossed and turned, and spoke some strange language in his sleep. The twins wore earbuds and stared at their laptops. I texted Molly, wishing her a good night; she sent back a heart emoji. I tiptoed to the patio and called my boss, expecting voicemail. But she answered. And fired me.

I washed, changed into pajamas and eased myself into bed. Sally breathed audibly, less than a snore but more than quiet. With the shades open, the full moon lit the wall where we kept our colorfully calligraphed *ketubah*, our ritual marriage contract. I remembered a hallucination from my first day of Covid delirium. Or maybe it was a dream. Sally, who became Molly, who became Eliana was showing me her scars. On the wrists. Behind her breasts. Red splotches on her knee. A thin blue line across her neck. A leprous, white, scaly patch under her arm. Ball-bearing tears flowing down her cheeks. Look! she said. Look! Look!